Viral Stories

Viral Stories

Cameron Dusting

Published internationally by Cam Dusting 2021

This book is a work of fiction. Any references to real people, real places, or historical events are used fictitiously. Other names, characters, places, and events are fictional, and any resemblance to actual events or places or persons, living or dead, is unintentional and coincidental.

The Tram first published at 'Fiction on the Web' 2019

Cascading Light and Sexual Eternity first published at 'Squawk Back' 2020

Copyright © 2021 by Cameron Dusting

All rights reserved. The purchaser of this book is subject to the condition that he/she shall in no way resell it, nor any part of it, nor make copies of it to distribute freely.

ISBN: 978-0994513021

Cover art copyright © 2021 by Maprang Jerachotiga

Cover design copyright © 2021 by Maprang Jerachotiga and Cameron Dusting

Introduction

Hi! I'm Cam and I travel while writing fiction. Thank you for reading! These stories are extremely different from one another. *The Tram* is a Czech woman's recollection of her formative experiences. *Ahead* follows two young men out on the town. *Vuiru Lake* is a fairy-tale for grownups. *Cascading Light and Sexual Eternity* portrays an altruist's rescue of another woman. This book's main feature is *Viral*, an action-packed story of a writer, a musician, and a comedian, all pursuing fame in the age of social media and COVID-19. *The Tram*, *Ahead*, *Vuiru Lake*, and *Cascading Light and Sexual Eternity* have all been popular online; until now, *Viral* has never been published. Though the stories are disconnected and unrelated, a note at the end of each story records where I was when I wrote it <3

Contents

The Tram   1

Ahead   11

Vuiru Lake   43

Cascading Light and Sexual Eternity   51

Viral   67

The Tram

The Tram

When I was nine years old, my family lived in a leafy district of Prague. My brother and sister and I went to school nearby; our mother would chat with the other parents by the school's metal fence while she waited for our classes to finish. After that, we'd walk home with her. It was a fifteen-minute walk under the leaves. Sometimes our friends and their parents would walk with us too. We'd pass the graffiti-covered buildings and the red-and-white railing, talking about what we'd learned at school that day.

On the walk home, my sister Kristýna, who was a year older than me, always complained about the wind getting in her hair. "So, tie it up," our mother would say. Krista's hair was honey-coloured; mine was much darker. We both had long hair. Yet the wind never bothered me. I loved feeling the breeze through my hair. It felt similar to my mother's fingers running over my scalp. On one such occasion, I spoke up. "I don't mind the wind in my hair," I said. And my mother laughed, and replied, "Of course you don't, Anna."

Then we'd arrive home, and our dachshund, Marek, would stand up to hug us and lick our faces. As soon as he'd calmed down, we'd change into looser clothes. We all had our own bedrooms, yet I remember a lot of time spent in the living room, which had large windows that looked out into our garden. We'd sit on the sofa with our arms around one another, watching *Pat & Mat* and *Večerníček* on the TV. Other times we'd play little games our mother would teach us. She had a way of turning any boring time into a fun one. She would find some paper and a pen, and transform them into something more: a puzzle, or a sort of template upon which, suddenly, anything seemed possible. When my mother's games failed to cure my boredom, I rarely let this show, because I'd feel terrible when I did.

Our father worked all the time. He was built like an athlete, and his smile was wide and charming. He owned a few beanies, but he usually wore his black one. Eventually, my little brother would resemble him.

We took for granted the fact that our mother played with us. We were kids. We couldn't have understood that since the Revolution (in which our parents, university students at the time, had demonstrated), Czechs had raised 'independent' children. We were no exception. When Kristýna and I bickered, our parents never broke up the fight — it was our brother who did that. But we couldn't have understood that many of our friends were growing up ignored. We were, and are, so fortunate never to have doubted our parents' love.

When the weather was right, we'd go cycling. The best places were outside the city. I vividly remember the five of us cycling through a scarlet poppy field on the way to a castle. The air smelt rich, if that's possible, and the sunlight was warm on our faces. I was filled with joy. Remembering the past, there's this sense that you know things now that you didn't know then — and that it was good before you found out. Growing up is good too. But that doesn't mean childhood isn't.

I know that not everyone likes Christmas, but I'm not ashamed to say that, of all the holidays in the Czech calendar, Christmas was always my favourite. I would look forward to it long in advance, and my brother and sister were the same. Every year, we'd set the tree up in the living room as early in December as our parents allowed us. We'd decorate its branches with glass balls, and ornaments made of straw. We'd make an Advent wreath with candles on it, and hang it outside the door to the house. Every year, around the 21st of December, our parents would bring home an enormous carp (though by the time I was nine, he already seemed smaller than I remembered). He lived in the bathtub, and everyone loved him, except my little brother, who was a little afraid of him. My brother wasn't afraid of much; maybe he was just wary of becoming too attached to the carp. Because, as we all knew, when Christmas dinner finally arrived, we ate him with soup, potato salad, bread, and honey—the fish, that is.

I was ten on the Thursday in autumn when it all changed. Our mother walked us to school, like any other day. She went to work, and on her lunchbreak, crossing Na Struze with a coffee in her hand, she was hit by a guy in his twenties. She just didn't see the car. It wasn't his fault; it wasn't her fault either. It was simply a second too early, or a second too late. It just happened.

So, when school ended that day, no one came to walk us home.

Our father chose to go on with life, and he inspired the three of us to do the same. His name is Michal; he's the strongest man I know. We understood that if he could have brought our mother back, he would have. And we understood that no one could do that. We grew up quickly. So, when we were in second stage and secondary school, we were okay when our father dated a lot of women. We met some of them. To this day, there's never been someone we've been close to calling our step-mother — but maybe someday, there will be.

After I graduated from secondary school, I studied Biology at Charles University. I lived in a dormitory and went home on the weekends. Through mutual friends, I met Jakub when I was twenty-one. I'm pretty tall, like the rest of my family, but I still have to look up to see him. Jakub has beautiful brown eyes, and golden-brown hair that falls below his ears. I was still with my ex-boyfriend when we started falling for each other, and it wasn't long before we were dating.

Life was really great. I was enjoying my Biology classes, and doing well in them too. The dorm I lived in was pretty quiet, but on the weekends I'd go out with Jakub, my sister Kristýna, and all of our friends. Krista and I ran in the same circles. I was close with both of my siblings, but my little brother just didn't run in our social circles. He was more introverted than us. I never met many of his friends. Besides, by this time, my little brother was studying abroad in Germany.

Prague is famous for its nightlife, and Krista and I were experts. On Friday and Saturday nights, we would meet at a friend's house to drink, before moving to a bar. Then, around midnight, we'd turn up at M1 or Vzorkovna, and we'd dance the night away. I wasn't a big fan of EDM; hip-hop and R&B were more my thing. I loved Rihanna. Krista and I took dancing classes in second stage. Jakub, on the other hand, dances like a monkey.

I thought I'd loved other boys before him. What I found with Jakub, though, was totally different. I honestly never thought I could love someone that much. Why would I ever want to take drugs, when I already had the best feeling in the universe?

My dorm had strict rules about guests, so Jakub never came over during the week. But we were together every single weekend. I remember being in my bedroom with him back then, just looking into his eyes. It was like the air had become water. Everything was shimmering, but I didn't have any tears.

"I can't believe it," I said to him that night.

"Believe it, Anna," he replied, in his clear voice.

My little brother was going to come home from Germany for Christmas. We all missed him and couldn't wait to see him again. It was all planned out; it all made sense.

And then, on the 19th of December 2016, he sent us all a message from Germany. He told us he was sorry. And he hanged himself in his closet.

It's been nearly two years since my baby brother's death—and nearly two and a half years since the last time we were with him. These two years have been the worst of my life. Of course they have. But lately, I can't help but to feel happy. Things are okay, really. I'm nearly twenty-four now. I still have Kristýna. I still have Jakub. I still have my dad. Our family has the absolute best, most loving, most supportive friends we could have ever imagined. It's not long until I'll finally have a degree in Biology. I don't know what I'll do after I graduate—but that's kind of exciting.

When we were kids, my baby brother would sleep-talk in the middle of the night. Our rooms shared a wall, and luckily for him I was the only one who'd hear it—if Kristýna had heard him murmuring away like that, she'd have teased him endlessly. I asked him what he was always dreaming about. But my little brother was always kind of secretive, and he wouldn't answer my question. I persisted, and finally, one day, he told me. He dreamed about a beach. He'd never seen the ocean. My little brother never liked Prague. He wanted to leave the city and swim at the beach. When he told me, I felt as though I'd been let in on a huge secret.

He got to swim at the beach in real life, eventually. I like to think he had a happy life. Our mother's death affected all of us, but it would be fair to say it affected him a little more. But I really think my brother was pretty happy for most of his twenty years. He just got unlucky toward the end. A few things happened in his personal life, unbeknownst to us. I believe it was only in the last year of his life that his depression started to take hold. Maybe we could have helped. Or maybe—and this is something I've been thinking about recently—we *did*. My family have always been extremely close. It may sound dark—but nowadays, I think that what happened was supposed to happen.

I used to spend so much time wishing I'd hung out more with my baby brother when he was alive. My mother, too. We all did—Michal, Kristýna, me—the three survivors. We spent so much time wishing we'd done things differently. But eventually, I stopped wishing. I just accepted that what happened happened. And then, things got better.

*

The Tram

Though I've never had a recurring dream—like my brother and his beach—once, when I was really young, I had a dream filled with autumn leaves. They floated in the wind and covered the pavements. They turned the entire city orange—this happens every year in Prague, but in the dream, it was even more so. We crunched over the leaves, breaking them. It was so much fun. We did this in real life, too—but in real life, I always wanted more leaves. In the dream, they were abundant.

Then we were in a playground, making huge piles out of the leaves, which were all shades of orange. The piles were so big that us kids could enter them, like rooms, so that we were totally submerged. All five of us played in the leaves, and my father nodded at passing strangers, and Krista swung on the swing.

My mother's name was Dana, and my brother's name was Petr. My mother was tall, with straight brown hair to her shoulders, and her face was small and sweet. At the time, my brother was the smallest in the family. He was a little bit chubby, too. He had his father's wide, charming smile.

In the dream, though, everyone's features were a little different. That's how dreams always are for me. Everyone looks a little different, but they're still themselves.

The entire time we played in the leaves, deep down I knew that our playing time was going to come to an end. That feeling was constant during the entire dream. At last, my mother said, "We're going to the tram, now." And I looked up, and she was walking away from us, hand-in-hand with my baby brother. Auburn leaves fell across their image as they walked away.

And then I woke up, and remembered that they were only asleep in their beds.

Prague
Dec 2018

Ahead

Ahead

It was one of those midsummer Friday nights when the city is alive and the wheels are rolling. You could see it in the cars that raced ahead, in the distant skyscrapers that loomed out of the darkness, along the road, in its painted strips that blurred when you looked at them so that they appeared instead as a single line. You could see it on the dark horizon, still visible despite the all-pervasive blackness. You could see it on the pulsing dashboard, in the colored lights of its buttons and precisely marked meters and the ring-shaped outlines of its dials. You could smell it in the cigarette smoke and you could hear it in the music, unrelenting, emanating from the speakers: *Do You Don't You* by Haywyre.

It was eight-thirty. Jesse's car shot down the highway—a steel bar magnetically attracted to the vast electric alnico of the metropolis ahead. All cars on the ten-lane highway shot—they all were steel bars. But the image was ruined when one in the next lane swerved, nearly colliding with Jesse's. Sitting in the seat that felt like a warm bath, Bruce Taylor, a young man with soft hair and a clean-shaven face, reacted: "Fucking asshole." He followed his words with a charming grin.

Jesse took down his window. Lukewarm air blasted the parts of Bruce's body that weren't blocked by Jesse, who screamed: "Hey! Fuck you!"

Bruce gazed ahead and enjoyed another of Jesse's rages. Jesse was bearded, and might have been compared to a hound dog—for while he lacked a tail, he possessed the beady eyes that told you his hungers were as simple as his thoughts. He furthermore raged the way a Basset Hound barked.

Bruce kept his distance from Jesse, who did the same.

Ahead

But when the night called, Bruce and Jesse always answered.

Jesse used his right hand to turn down the banger banging on repeat. "Jesus Christ," he was saying. "What the fuck is wrong with these drivers?"

He didn't expect nor receive a reply. He took his window up. Now the beat pumped at a reasonable volume—but the beat pumped on.

"That's fucking beautiful man," said Bruce after some time.

"I know man," replied Jesse.

They surveyed the skyscrapers up ahead.

"It's like a blinking, beautiful thing. It's like lights, but they're not shining on me, you know what I mean? They're blinking, but they're not looking at me. It's like… they know what's up." Jesse was speaking; now he laughed. "They know how it is."

"I mean, there's nothing like it." Bruce spoke now. "Here we are on the road. And up ahead are the skyscrapers. They call us."

"They're not looking at me," said Jesse.

"They're not looking at you," agreed Bruce. "But they know we're headed for them. They're asking us to join them. They're magnificent. They twinkle with the light of ten thousand people. Can you imagine that each tiny window is a person? A human life."

Jesse looked at Bruce. "What?"

"I said the windows are people," answered Bruce.

Jesse paused. "Ok man. There are people in the windows."

"The people *are* the windows," amended Bruce. "Some you've met, others you haven't. But they're all together, all up there, all around us." Their highway was flanked by the city's skyscrapers;

surrounded. "And they're dazzling." They dazzled Bruce, anyway.

"Some are white, some are red, some are blue," tried Jesse. "But they're all people."

Bruce turned to Jesse. "No they're not. Those aren't windows."

Jesse peered up at one of the red lights crowning a nearby skyscraper: an aircraft warning light. "Same shit."

Bruce went on: "They're breathing, man. They're alive. They're calling us from above. They're extending an offer to take us up, to where fluorescent ceiling lights are chopped up by the bits of wall separating windows of the same room."

"There are two hundred and eighty-six windows up there." Jesse up-nodded the space to his left, where there lay a vast expanse populated by overlapping grids of windows; some dim, others lined, some revealing dots within, and others softly glowing. "Two hundred and eighty-six of our friends, welcoming us warmly into their midst."

"Did you fucking count them?" demanded Bruce, grinning.

"They glimmer. They light up the skies. They light up our lives! They dance yellow now, all around us like a happy constellation of human stars," went on Jesse.

"The city's a royal family, and a good one. In fact, it's a dynastic noble clan of multistoried high-rise buildings, adorned, as they are, in robes patterned with tiny squares of gold. And the kings and queens!: crowned with electric crowns, neon brand logos, and hyper-intelligent viridescent headdresses from the technologically advanced future, which teach them facts such as the chemical compositions of the planets."

"Shut the fuck up!" snorted Jesse. "Which planets?"

"The fucking planets of the solar system!" yelled Bruce.

"And all two thousand seven hundred and sixty-seven exoplanetary systems?" demanded Jesse.

"What the fuck!" exclaimed Bruce, shocked. He laughed.

"Fuuuuck," growled Jesse. He took down the front two windows; air roared. He opened the roof. They flew ahead.

"So blurry," yelled Bruce at last. "They're not... shaped like lights..."

"Nothing is," returned Jesse. They'd arrived downtown. Jesse took a violent left, mimicking the tire squeal with a fiendish howl into the night air. These echoed along the street's walls.

Grinning, Bruce wondered whether he'd heard Jesse correctly. "*Nothing is*"? Say what? Jesse hit the volume and they were engulfed once again. The banger filled the street, it turned heads containing amazed faces. Unconsciously nodding, Bruce realized that for once in Jesse's life, he was right. Nothing was shaped like lights: nothing was good. Bruce was happy, so happy, but he knew this was owed solely to the MDMA that moved through his blood. Surrounded by the halos of the streetlights, the warm evening air making love to his clean-shaven face, his exposed chest, Bruce Taylor forced himself not to recall Olivia's face. Now was not the time.

Soon they were behind one of those windows in the sky. An apartment with dozens of people they loved; people who loved them back. Jesse hit the balcony, crowded as usual; seeing this, Bruce, wearing his yellow Hawaiian shirt, cruised instead into Theo and Kory's room. Kory and three homies sat on Kory's bed and the seat adjacent. They yelled with joy at the yellow sight of Bruce, who collapsed onto their bodies, hugging and laughing. Someone forced a wet pair of beer cans into Bruce's hands. Eventually he took a seat on the free bed, Theo's, standing the cans on the carpet, rolling a cigarette. He was lost in concentration, seeming to float on the bed's softness, when Renee neared. She said his name, and he looked up, startled; quickly he smiled, welcoming her into his arms. They talked for a long time, who knew how long?, and watched as their friend Sam destroyed a small table with his foot. It was probably Theo's table; or, it had been.

Renee secretly loved Bruce. But now Yosan caught Bruce's eye; and, setting his open beer upon the closest available surface—Theo's comforter—Bruce danced with his right shoulder, the one Renee didn't occupy. Between thick curtains of curly red hair, Yosan smiled gorgeously, large eyes down, swaying her hips right and left to the beat of the music. But she remained where she was, beyond the door to the living room; now she looked Bruce in the eyes again, beckoning him with graceful upward sweeps of her arms. Bruce hesitated. Renee, leaning into him, held her breath. Bruce's cheeky, adorable grin awoke in Renee irrepressible laughter, as simultaneously her heart sunk. Bruce let go of Renee's body, standing to accept Yosan's offer.

"He-ey," Yosan called.

Bruce danced into the loud living room, kissed Yosan's cheek, joined her in dance. Yosan handed Bruce a half bottle of vodka; Bruce accepted thirstily, reveling in its burn. They danced body to body, Yosan's legs either side of Bruce's thigh. They went like this for some time, Yosan grinding exquisitely against Bruce's right thigh, steps synchronized; their union attracted eyes, friend's' exclamations, strangers' smiles.

At last he fell into Yosan's kiss; it was like diving headfirst into an oddly warm sea. But quickly he withdrew, took a step back. They were surrounded by friends.

Bruce thought of Jesse, who never had trouble convincing each of his girlfriends that they were, in his exact words, *"The only girl for me"*. Wherever Jesse was, Bruce guessed he was probably consoling one of his girlfriends. Bruce had always felt for them, especially the few he'd met. The poor things. How could they be so blind? Bruce rarely lied, he never cheated. Now single, in past relationships he'd been cheated on; yet he'd never cheated. He'd always restrained himself. He didn't like to lead people on.

"I think we should take this to Charlie's room," said Yosan, voice emitting like beeps.

"Aren't you going to the club?" asked Bruce, confused. He'd thought the plan had been to mob to a nightclub some of their crowd frequented.

"I mean, I guess…" said Yosan, lips swiveling.

"Where the fuck is Jesse though?" said Bruce, looking past Yosan, scanning the glowing living room.

"Dude, fuck that dude," said Yosan. She watched as Bruce retrieved his phone. "I don't really know why you hang out with him…"

Bruce knew that everything was cool—even if twenty-five years hadn't taught Jesse empathy, he was a grown man who could take care of himself… but then again, was he? Bruce knew that from cuts and food-poisonings, all the way to drug overdoses and serious brawl-related injuries, Jesse had been hospitalized every year since high school. Tonight wasn't going to be one of those nights. He had enough shit on his mind.

"I gotta find Jesse," said Bruce, deaf to Yosan's mutters. Phone to his ear, he looked at her wide brown eyes. "I'll be back. Sorry." And he meant it.

He returned to Theo's room, put his phone volume on full, concentrated on the dialing noise. *Zzzhhhp zzzhhhp.* Jesse took a few minutes to answer.

"Yo," he barked.

Bruce yelled.

"Where the fuck are you?"

Their gang of twenty dominated the train-car; the ride was one for the ages. Bruce sat with Kandice, whose lively face on weekend nights was kept clear by the blonde ponytail tight atop her head; and Tuuli, who for all the years he'd known her, had never altered her wavy, dark brown cascade, nor lost the understated smile it framed. Theo, Sam, Mickey, JP, Mason, and Lena stood in the aisle, packing it, yelling, lit; entertaining Bruce, Kandice, Tuuli, and the rest of their group, sprawled across the seats; throwing a hackey-sack across one another, intimidating wary onlookers. When they rolled up at the metro station, they hooted and hollered, running onto the crowded platform and up the escalator, spilling out into the dark. Night-people populated the wide boulevard, their yells echoing down its shop-front walls. Someone sprinted, cut through the middle of their crowd; Mickey turned, screamed madly after him. They mobbed down the boulevard toward their destination: the large nightclub containing Jesse, Jesse's pack, and hordes of clubbers.

Of course the bouncer asked for proof of Bruce's age. Floating, discarding his cigarette, as usual he took this as a compliment; added to this the fact that seconds before, Mickey had stuck a middle finger inches behind the bouncer's oblivious head, upon entry Bruce flashed the bouncer a warm smile and a "Thanks bruh I appreciate it man." And he did appreciate it. The bouncer couldn't have been enjoying his night, dealing with an endless stream of fuckheads, standing on the street as the hours brought the cold...

Inside. Glowing blue. Kandice and Tuuli inside, less than five seconds. To the bar. Kandice and Tuuli agreed: drinks, the one thing more important than finding Jesse. He was somewhere in here. Stepping past a group of screaming, hugging young women. A gang of guys huddled around tables. A huge, scary man dancing with closed eyes. A couple making out, the woman's arms around the man's neck, the man's hands shamelessly massaging the woman's ass-cheeks. "Damn," shouted Bruce over the earth-shattering electronic music. Kandice and Tuuli laughed in unison.

"What do you want?" Bruce asked Kandice, eyeing the bearded barman through the thirsting mass as Tuuli weaved straight into it.

"Whatever you're having," answered Kandice, predictably.

Tuuli turned around abruptly, flicking wavy hair, beckoning Bruce and Kandice. Wearing the most seductive of her facial expressions, she held the attention of the youngest barman, easily underage. They squeezed through, affecting apology, arriving at the front.

"Ask him to tell you what you're thinking," Tuuli, pouting, said to Bruce.

"Oohh!" exclaimed Bruce as Kandice laughed. "What am I thinking?"

The boy tore his eyes off Tuuli, stared at Bruce.

"You're tryna get fucked up!"—at least, that's what Bruce thought he heard.

A homie handshake, tight over the wooden bar: "My man! My man."

The kid poured three whiskey shots. "On me. Anything else y'all were after?"

"Three pitchers of Bud," said Tuuli, lingering teasingly on the last word.

The wide-eyed kid grinned. "I gotchu."

Taps on Bruce's shoulder: "I don't want that." Kandice pointed at the whiskey. "You want it?"

"I mean, yeah," answered Bruce automatically. He leaned to Tuuli's ear: "Do you want Kandi's shot?"

"I can't." Tuuli smiled. "Anyway, you need it."

Tuuli was right. She was one of the few who knew.

Kid busy at Budweiser tap. Clinking two shot glasses against Tuuli's. Fingers whiskey-wet. Head back. Throat stinging… throat stinging twice.

DJ screaming over system. Beat drop. Hundreds of shaded clubbers, ghosts of glory, going at it. Four of Bruce's friends among them. He couldn't fuck with that right now. Dancing over to reserved table—purple shirt buttoned all the way up, skinny navy jeans—Budweiser pitcher heavy under hanging fingers, Kandice at side. Sitting. Gazing at bottle-stuffed ice bucket.

"Bruce!"

Theo. Kissing Bruce's cheek. Prickly. Ouch. Smacking off it. Ouch!

"My brother," said Bruce, throaty, high-pitched.

"I feel like I haven't seen you in forever dude!" said Theo, greasy shoulder-length hair cutting through blue.

"I mean, we were just at your house," said Bruce.

Theo's toasted brain recollected; his pale face opened. It grew taller. Turned away. Slammed down with each beat. Hair grease up-spit, refracting blue light.

Right arm hanging on to Theo's sweaty shoulders. Left hand pulling out phone. Messages from Jesse. Shit! Jesse!

"*11:04pm*

Bathroom"

"*11:10pm*

Bathroom"

Jesse was in the bathroom. That meant the fucker had coke. Bruce didn't need that right now. Neither did Jesse; but that was

Jesse's problem. Locking phone. Left leg out. Slipping phone in pocket…

…ripping bottles from bucket. Mixing red juice and gin in glass. Neat. Downing it. Pouring another, same again. Downing it… turning. Behind, above, friends dancing on ledge. Women only. Hands in the air, hair flicking, hips pulsing. Anastasia bending her knees. Facing away. Oh shit. Quinn bending her knees. Lena: "Get it giiirl!" Anastasia and Quinn's huge asses a-twerk. Quinn gazing over her shoulder at Bruce. Ass up and down with the beat. Bruce exaggerating a face of approval.

A lull.

Familiar music.

"OooooohhhhHHHHHHH!!" screamed the group. Standing. Bottle pourers stabbing leg, stabbing crotch. Ouch! Pushing; bottle-overflowing steel bucket sliding away. Glass smashing on wooden floor. Someone else did it.

"*THERE'S NO WAY I COULD TURN YOU DOWN! WHEN I KNOW THAT THERE'S A CHANCE TO SHOW YOU!*" They know the lyrics. Everyone in the club knows they know the lyrics. Eyes closed. Arms locked on shoulders; Kandice to his left, Theo to his right. Friends behind, above. Twisting hips. Jumping. "*BUT IF ONLY I COULD LET THIS OUT! I COULD LET THIS OUT!*"

Beat drop. Dry ice. Confetti! Smile exploding. Letting go of Theo to pound the space above, which Bruce knew contained all of his repressed sadness; punching the absolute fuck out of fog, sad billowing fog, grinning at it, hard as physically possible. Mind cascading. Everything blue, lifting. Grin wide, beautiful. Staring up. Friends lining peripheral. Blue twinkling outward like water. Wow. Feels good. Harder.

If there was ever a song to make Bruce fist-pump, it was *Shy* by The Magician.

Light-headed. Nightclub twinkling, clubbing ghosts flashing in and out of vision: light on off on off on off. Confetti dotting down. Twinkling Theo on the circular table: his boy since high school. Theo wild, spinning his head, shaking it spastically. Hair grease spitting like a fry pan on high heat. Theo's steps: kicks. Kicking glasses down. Glass exploding. Liquid spreading, dripping. Theo out of control. Holy fuck. To Bruce's right, Louise, uncomfortable. She saw Bruce's concern, darted out of their ring-booth, danced nearby with her big homie, Addy… Louise was safe, outside Theo's blast range. Inevitably, two guards ducked under Theo's outstretched arms, hauled Theo off the table. Bruce stepped, crunching broken glass, around the table's circumference. "Get the fuck off him!" A hard look. A firm push to Bruce's purple-shirted chest. Back. Sam and Mickey hot on the guards' heels. A typical Friday. Better enjoy the club while he still could. Bruce lifted his arms. Banged his head. Felt deliciously sad and happy at the same time.

The song lowered now. Bruce stared at the ground, noticed how dizzy he was. His shoes clicked to the bottom edge of his visual field, over and over again. Amazing. But Theo was gone. So were Sam and Mickey. Always. Uh. Stamping his foot. Hard. Kill the floor. Olivia's face seemed to emerge into the sparkling dark. No. Bruce shoved the image out of his frazzled consciousness. Out. Away. Not now. He felt his throat tighten. He focused on the song, the saddest song in the world. The song that danced across the distant walls of the club, controlling the blue ghost-bodies inside, ricocheting off the barely visible ceiling.

Arm around his shoulder. Female's. Voice in his left ear.

"Have you got any coke?"

Kandice.

"No, but um, I think Jesse... might..." slurred Bruce.

Kandice stared at Bruce. Eyes wide. Still.

"I don't know where he is, is the thing..." He slid his phone out. Messages. Missed calls. Jesse.

"*11:17pm*

Where you"

"*11:17pm*

Bruce"

"*11:28pm*

Fucking where are you. Call me"

There was more. But Bruce stopped reading. He stared down at the blinding white screen. He was coming down. All around him, molly's magic died faster than Jesse's preferred driving speed. So it was that at some lost moment, Bruce's joy had transformed into a cold pointlessness that sat in his stomach, in front of his unfocused eyes... he deliberately kept these unfocused. He made out the blurred light of his phone screen. So bright. He wanted it to blind him. He didn't want to see.

"Are you alright?" inquired Kandice to his left.

"Yeah, I'm good," said Bruce, eyes focusing, reading. "You want to get some coke?"

Kandice's face lit up. "Has Jesse got it?"

"Yeah," said Bruce. "He's in the hills."

"How's your night going?" Bruce asked the Uber driver.

"It's fucking crazy out here," came a rasp from under the oversized brim of a cowboy hat.

Caught off guard, Bruce said, "Yeah?"

"It's wild," rasped the driver. "People out here are on one, my friend."

Bruce laughed: mouth stale, face pale. With any luck, the drive wasn't going to kill him. It wasn't long before he'd be coming up on the night's second dose of MDMA: he'd swallowed another two caps as soon as the effects of the first two wore off. Bruce looked behind at Kandice sitting in the back seat. He had to make sure she was okay; he was pleased to see her sweaty smile. The plan was to meet Jesse at some famous person's party. "*Some famous person's party*"—that was all the information Jesse had given.

"You smoke?" asked the driver.

"Yeah," replied Bruce.

"Think I've got a little…"

The driver fumbled around his door, producing a joint literally the size of a drumstick.

Bruce and Kandice screamed, exchanging droop-eyed gapes; were they dreaming?

"AYAYAYAY," roared the driver, starting and stopping the car's acceleration. The car kicked forward, the dark street jerked up and down before Bruce's eyes… the cowboy hat flopped forward and back: underneath, the driver's grin stretched away, immortal. "I'M KOWBOY KOOL! WELCOME TO MY

CAR!" He max-volumed the EDM with his right hand; with his left, he held out the joint, the paper drumstick, to Bruce. Bruce accepted it immediately, anxious to free Kowboy Kool a hand for the steering wheel.

"THERE SHOULD BE A LIGHTER!" Kowboy Kool pointed at the glove compartment.

"Wow man," yelled Bruce. "I'm Bruce, this is Kandice!"

"PLEASURE TO MEET YOU BRUCE, CANNABIS!" beamed Kowboy Kool.

Bruce snorted, lighting up. Behind Kandice yelled: "Did you just call me cannabis?"

"YES HONEY! THAT'S YOUR NAME RIGHT?"

After a pause, Kandice laughed: "I mean, sure!"

Bruce took several deep drags, before surrendering the hefty thing back to Kandice, who sat puffing away beside her open window. It wasn't long before Kowboy Kool was offering them the rest of his goods: acid, coke, molly, bars. Speed. Ketamine, even. For a price, of course: but they were happy to pay. Bruce trusted the guy's eyes; and he'd come down, so he trusted his trust, too. He didn't plan to eat any more molly caps that night. So he bought a single acid blotter from Kowboy Kool.

"THAT'S THE GOOD STUFF!" assured the chirpy cowboy.

"Appreciate it," said Bruce. He yelled back to Kandice: "Yo, I wouldn't rely on Jesse for your coke."

Kandice leaned forward to breathe into Bruce's ear. "Doesn't he have it?"

"He said so," said Bruce in hers. "But it's Jesse." He shrugged animatedly: Kandice got the message. Bruce leaned around again. "This guy's selling fifty-dollar grams."

"Driver! Can I get a gram of coke?" yelled Kandice.

"YEEAAAH MAAANN!" was the reply.

The car smelt dank, despite the fact that Kandice's window was open. Bruce relaxed against his headrest, breathing deeply, staring cutely through the glass of his own. The dark headlight-shooting streets grew wider, the buildings shrunk. Now the avenues were lined with towering palms. He placed the LSD under his tongue. He forced the sadness down, away, willing the MDMA to hit him faster. He'd politely declined the driver's joint-pass; now Kandice held it under his nose from behind. "I'm good, I'm good," Bruce said, turning around so Kandice could hear. "I don't wanna get too faded." He already felt faded. He couldn't completely zone out; he had to be present, aware. But Kandice held the joint still, right below his nose.

"C'mon," Kandice urged.

"I'm good Kandice," said Bruce, ignoring the thick smoke wafting up into his eyes.

"Dude…" yelled Kandice. She held it for another few seconds but Bruce stared stubbornly out his window. Kandice sighed, trying to elicit Bruce's guilt; she passed the thing across to the cheerful, scream-rasping, party-drug-slinging cowboy.

Bruce and Kandice fell into silence. Kowboy Kool made strange percussive noises with his throat and mouth, accentuating the music, grinning all the while. Bruce smiled faintly out at the streets. His phone buzzed. He pulled it out.

"12:30am

What's wrong?"

That had been Kandice. Bruce locked his phone and stared out the window again, letting the blaring music roll over him. He grew irritated at the driver's noises. He was drunk as hell, significantly stoned, and suffering the empty, life-is-meaningless feeling at the tail end of a molly high, that let-down, which time after time he'd deny and deny, refusing to believe. But soon, the second pair of capsules would take him back. Bruce thought of Jesse, empty-eyed Jesse; Bruce needed to see him. Tall and skinny, Jesse was probably entertaining a beautiful group of women right now, or selling coke to celebrities, or else breakdancing inside a circle of bewildered strangers. There was no one like Jesse. And somehow, nobody seemed to give Bruce advice as good as Jesse's. Apart from Jesse, there was only one person whose presence could make Bruce happy right now… but she was not an option. She wasn't here. (He'd told Tuuli what had happened. But he'd asked her not to tell anyone yet. He knew he could trust Tuuli. Kandice clearly didn't know—and that was as much proof of Tuuli's loyalty as Bruce could ever hope for.) So, Jesse it was. Plus, he really should be keeping the kid from trouble. Bruce willed the fake cowboy to drive harder, willed his body to digest faster. He re-opened his phone, lowered the screen's brightness setting, and replied Kandice's message, taking great care with his wording.

"12:37am

Just been not great lately. Personal stuff. I appreciate your kindness homie. Sorry if I come across as rude or anything"

He sent the message; and looked up, out the window, to meet the glorious sight of a mansion; the image stayed frozen in Bruce's mind after the Uber had zoomed past. Red and white, round pillars; early twentieth century, Catalan modernist, Bruce guessed. So, they'd arrived in the poor part of town. Refocusing, Bruce saw through trees a steely-silver driveway, rolling up endlessly... an ugly grey and green brick-shaped mansion... an enormous leafy hedge wall... and then they were on a one-way street, on the way up, and... Oh damn! So was he! By God, so was he. He must have been on the way up for minutes.

He felt Kandice's hand on his right shoulder. Squeezing... it felt good. Bruce loved Kandice as a friend and maybe as more. Kandice was hilarious, so much fun to be around, always down to party—but Kandice was deep too, and late at night could engage Bruce in heavy conversation, and might even become over-serious. Bruce loved this about Kandice. But he thought of Yosan. He felt guilty. At Theo's apartment, he'd led Yosan on more than he would've liked. Renee, too. And what would Olivia think of all this?... Well, again, she wasn't here. So Bruce stayed still, allowing Kandice to comfort him, allowing himself to be comforted by Kandice, gazing out the window as the Uber climbed higher and higher, winding through the hills at break-neck speed.

Jesse's text had instructed Bruce and Kandice to enter *"through the front door"*. But Kowboy Kool had dropped them off on a corner, at the bottom of at least fifty stone steps: a mailbox proved the address correct. They couldn't be sure to which properties the nearest driveways belonged; but more electronic music pumped, distant; and another couple climbed the stairway, way ahead, way above. There'd been a slight cool change. Bruce extended his left arm, letting Kandice snuggle into his side. His left arm wrapped around her back; he held her body to his. Cosy in their newfound closeness, they began the ascent like this.

A breeze blew, rustling the leaves on their sides.

"I'm scared," said Kandice.

"Don't be," said Bruce.

They ascended in silence. Bruce wore black shoes and slacks, and a black coat and tie over a freshly ironed white shirt. Kandice wore a tight-hugging navy-blue dress that extended to her calves; plain, but for a crisscross pattern over her chest. The cool breeze blew at their skin. With each step, the pumping grew louder.

"This is really fucking nice though," said Kandice.

Far above the road, at last they arrived on an open concrete landing framed by exotic trees. Dozens of formally-dressed people stood around in groups; drinking, smoking, laughing. But Bruce barely noticed them, for backgrounding them was a mansion unlike anything he could ever have imagined. Silver and steely-grey, like a space station; though Bruce saw it was made of concrete and stone, wood and gleaming glass. Two immense wooden structures stood erect—octagonal or dodecagonal prisms, or something; pillars, or towers, made of hundreds of horizontal grey wooden planks and inlayed with immaculate sheets of glass, behind which stood more formally-dressed night-people, drinking and laughing; some gazed down their noses into the landing. Silver Italian marble inlayed with more glass windows connected these pillars; to the sides stood concrete walls, emblazoned by outdoor lights glowing upward from pebbled strips on the ground. The whole thing hummed like a space station; surely plenty of its inhabitants were taking off right now. Bruce himself felt just about ready to board.

"I guess this is the front door," said Kandice.

Bruce laughed. Luckily he'd been in many a similar situation, and rather than nervous, he felt exhilarated, as beautiful as the surroundings. But he had to make sure Kandice felt the same. "Are you good?" He looked at her.

"Of course man!" said Kandice. "Are you?"

"Yeah."

"Alright, let's do it!"

They approached a gigantic doorman standing outside an equally gigantic steel door.

"Names," stated the doorman.

"I don't think we're on the list," said Bruce. "But Jesse Henderson's expecting us."

The doorman paused. Suddenly he exclaimed, "Oh you're Jesse's people!"

Bruce and Kandice smiled silently.

"Get in here!" The doorman pressed a button, causing the steel door to open wide; he gestured with an outstretched arm. He actually bowed. Smiling, arms interlocked, Bruce and Kandice stepped up onto the glass threshold, walking between the fire-spurting burners flanking the steel door. They sauntered through the doorway into the warmly-lit entrance hall, empty but for less than fifteen people, dressed to impress, yelling and joking; couples occupied the couches lining the walls. At least two of the couples made out. A staircase spiraled up into a loft; when Bruce looked up he lost himself to awe; the ceiling had to be at least thirty feet high.

"You wanna wait for me outside the bathroom?" said Kandice, eager to powder her nose.

"Sure," said Bruce. "But don't be too long. It'll take forever to find Jesse in this place." In search of a bathroom they walked through the entrance hall into an enormous living room. A group fought in there; quickly Bruce and Kandice walked behind a standalone wall, entering a hallway.

"Woah," said Kandice.

Between tapestries and magnificent artefacts lining the walls, eight doors were visible.

"One of these has to be a bathroom," said Bruce.

They took the first door to the right. It opened onto the entrance hall. Everyone in the room carried on socializing, making out; no one noticed Bruce and Kandice, who went back the way they came, this time taking the opposite door. Inside: a staircase leading down. It appeared to lead to the pumping music's source. Kandice descended into the noise, turning to Bruce: "C'mon!" Bruce hesitated; he followed.

The place was a fucking labyrinth; at the bottom of the wooden staircase were more than thirty attractive people in a huge bedroom. One of the walls was entirely glass; but a good-looking fella blocked the view. He smiled at the sight of Bruce and Kandice.

"Hey man, do you know if there's a bathroom nearby?" asked Bruce.

"Right over there!" declared the charming fella, pointing at a large pair of red-and-gold doors. "Walk through, make a left!"

"Thanks bruh."

Bruce and Kandice opened the red-and-gold doors, one each. Now they were in another living room; this time it featured a twenty-foot painting of... well, there was no other way to put it... of an Ancient Roman orgy. "Holy fuck," said Bruce.

"What the actual fuck," said Kandice. "I'm not high enough for this."

The room to the left, thank God, was a small bathroom.

Bruce stood outside as Kandice closed the door behind her, ignoring the lock. Now to find Jesse. He reached for his phone... but a sound distracted him. He turned around in search of its source; all he saw was an archway, under which he glided; and to his left he witnessed a basketball gymnasium, inside of which a hundred finely-clad people watched two armored knights atop horses. Bruce stared in disbelief; the black horses stood on either side of a fold-out fence that had been set up down the middle of the basketball court, in the floor of which sat crater-like holes and cracks. This was not a hallucination. For several minutes Bruce gaped... his trance was broken at the sound of his name.

"Bruce!"

He turned to see an elderly lady he did not recognize immediately. She smiled at him crazily, giving him no choice but to smile back... but of course, it was the librarian from his elementary school. Jesus Christ, what in the name of fuck was going on?

"Bruce Taylor, and how are you this evening?"

"Oh, I'm good!" said Bruce. "What the fuck is this?" He pointed to the horse-riding knights.

"Oh, well it's the joust, and pardon your language!" said the librarian, whose name Bruce failed to recall. "Yes, and it's just so much fun to watch!"

They watched the knights in silence for a minute. The tiny librarian repeated, "And how are you?"

"Oh, I'm great!" said Bruce. "And you?"

"Yes!" replied the librarian.

A painful silence; until the librarian began to explain the rules of jousting. Bruce bent to hear her words over the raucous yells of the suit- and dress-clad crowd. Ten minutes later the black horses were at either end of the basketball court; the crowd hushed rapidly. "Look, here they go," said the librarian, her tone focused, measured. Mounted on the horses, the knights pointed twelve-foot lances at one another. The entire room stopped, silent. The horses trotted, and then galloped toward one another; in a flash one of the knights was off the horse, smashing onto the polished wood of the court. The crowd exploded!, screaming, whistling. At least five of its members uncorked champagne bottles; foam sprayed over their heads.

"Hehehe, isn't it great?" said the librarian, foam in eye, looking on with crossed arms.

"It's pretty good," said Bruce; but his phone rang.

He pulled it out. Kandice. Shit.

"Hey sorry, I got totally sidetr-"

"Dude, where is Jesse?" Kandice interjected. "I really need Jesse. It's an emergency…"

"What happened?" asked Bruce, startled.

"I need more coke. N- not for me, but this girl needs coke and she's gonna fucking kill me if I can't get her any!"

"Are you serious right now?" yelled Bruce.

"Bruce, I'm dead serious. I'm out of coke. I'm in the bathroom… I need Jesse…"

"Alright I'm gonna help you," said Bruce, trying to remain calm. "I'm gonna help you as fast as I can." He hung up and called Jesse, leaving the librarian giggling in the gymnasium, soaring back through the archway. Bruce tried his best to block the just-witnessed scene from his memory, to focus. Ahead, on the far wall of the enormous living room, was the painting of the Roman orgy (was the living room enormous? Or was he tripping?). To the right was the red-and-gold double doorway. To the left of this, in the same wall as the orgy painting, was a door; to the right, an identical door. One of the two led to the bathroom he'd left Kandice in. But he couldn't remember which. Tucking his phone in between his ear and shoulder—it still waited on Jesse—he stretched his arms out to the sides like an albatross, managing to open both doors with a hand each.

A warm wind blew from the left, as did the electronic music's full blast; Bruce immediately looked to his right. Inside, a tall woman with waist-length, straight brown hair stood in front of a bathroom mirror; a nasty face, glaring at Bruce, curled over her shoulder. The mirror reflected Kandice, terrified.

"You didn't even lock the door?" yelled Bruce, hurling himself onto the tall brunette, phone clattering to the tiles. Bruce had been involved in many an altercation; never with a woman, though he gave no second thought to Kandice's attacker's gender. Faster than lightning he reached around to the attacker's right hand, where, he correctly predicted, she held a knife to Kandice's throat. Bruce didn't care if he got cut. He was euphoric, he was on fire. He wrenched the knife away from Kandice's throat, holding it (and the attacker's hand) outstretched, successfully locking the attacker in a half nelson with his left arm. She reached behind, pulling his hair; he tried to drag her backwards, away from Kandice. Kandice wriggled free, stammered into Bruce's phone. The attacker bent her right wrist, slicing Bruce's knuckle; he yelled but regained control of the attacker's hand immediately. He wrapped his right leg around that of the attacker; supported by a flimsy high-heel, the attacker thereby lost balance as Bruce kicked, cracking the wooden closet under the basin.

"You done?" he said.

"Get off me… you fucking animal!" she screamed hoarsely.

Bruce jumped backwards, heaving her gnarled body with him. Outside the bathroom, a group had gathered. Bruce immediately felt a draining sensation. "Shit."

"He's got her!" said a middle-aged man's voice.

"Get that thing out of here," snarled a woman's.

In the space between the two doors, Bruce froze, looking around. No one intervened.

"LET GO OF ME!" the woman screamed, harsh, voice breaking.

"She has a knife," Bruce said, panting. "In her… right hand."

"I gotchu homie," barked a familiar voice.

And standing there under the archway was none other than Bruce's knight in shining armor, helmet in hand. Gleaming, bearded, smiling. The one and only Jesse Henderson.

"DUDE!" said Bruce. Somehow, it made total sense that Jesse had competed in the joust. Bruce had never been happier to see him.

Jesse, decked out in lustrous Medieval English plate armor, towered over everyone else in the room. He stepped over, tore the knife right out of the hysterical woman's hand, stabbed it into the upper section of his steel plateleg. The tiny blade collapsed… the group cheered!

Two large security guards had arrived. Glancing briefly at Jesse under the archway—"Get back in the gym Jesse!"—each took the tall brunette by an arm. By now she sounded like a broken record: "Just let me have some coke. Just need some of that coke. You got any coke?" Soon, Bruce was assured, the guards had escorted her from the building.

The song pumping directly outside was *Shooting Stars* by Bag Raiders. Do you know that song? The song from that Internet meme where Donald Trump travels through space? Around February 2017, it was, when that meme was doing its rounds on the Internet. That song that might get on your nerves, even irritate the hell out of you, or might on the other hand make you feel like the entire world is collapsing right before your very eyes, all around you wherever you happen to be at that point in time.

Leaving Jesse with an admiring group of women, Bruce floated out into the warm night; he stood on a marble patio—a silver launch pad—surrounded by a colossal and jungle-like garden, featuring a flat and rainbow-lit infinity pool... radiant fountains in and around this, their psychedelic light illuminating grand statues of marble and glass... dual circular seating areas, filled with laughers; plush, sunk into the ground... rows and rows of flaming burners... and at least three hundred formally-dressed, glow-eyed night-people, dancing over tiled patios and barefoot on grass.

Kandice sat alone at the end of a corner-shaped outdoor sofa, far away to Bruce's left. As Bruce glided toward her, he saw her staring intently into the flame strip burning between them. If Kandice was about to get heavy on him, Bruce was prepared, and saw she'd released her blonde hair from its ponytail. She looked up. She smiled; the jungle-garden seemed to melt. Her smile deepened... this signaled the end of the world. She stood. Stepped around the flames. Held out her arms.

Bruce took her in his own...

"I'm safe."

"You're safe."

...and Bruce and Kandice had lifted off of the launch pad of the steely-silver space station in the hills. Together, they flew through space. Up, and up, and up. At last the song reached its summit and Bruce knew he'd reached his. It was the end. The universe collapsed... and Bruce and Kandice were all that remained.

Jesse's bark brought them back down to Earth.

"Hey!"

The Basset Hound held out his cigarette pack; Bruce and Kandice took one each.

"What happened to those girls?" asked Bruce.

Jesse merely shrugged and smoked.

"I saw the joust, by the way," said Bruce. "Fucking hell man. You lost right? Are you alive?"

"I fucking won!" barked Jesse. "I won!"

"Jesus," said Bruce. "Is the other guy alive?"

"No, he died," answered Jesse.

Bruce quickly decided he didn't want to find out whether this was a fact.

"You know I had that though," said Bruce, lifting his cigarette between towel-bandaged fingers.

Jesse howled. "C'mon man! She was gonna kill you! You would've been dead."

"Like, I appreciate your looking out for me, but it was all good…"

"Nah," said Kandice. "You would've been dead."

"Fuck you," said Bruce as Jesse howled. "It's not like I just saved your life…"

"C'mon, I'm only joking," said Kandice, rubbing Bruce's arm. "Thank you, Bruce. And you, too, Jesse." Her face was ghostly: she was out of cocaine. "I need some water. I'll be back."

"Holler at us before you go to the bathroom!" said Bruce, eyes serious.

Kandice laughed. "I'll be right here." She walked off toward one of the sunken seating disks, in the center of which lay a crystal ice bowl, packed with water bottles. Several people in the disk turned to smile at Kandice, welcoming her; she was within view, but out of earshot.

"Your mother would be proud," said Jesse.

And in a flood, her smiling face appeared, ahead, her bright face, laughing. It was only in Bruce's mind. But it overwhelmed him. Olivia's beautiful face, the happiest and the saddest thing in the world. Dead. Stroke, last Tuesday. Gone, forever. Laughing forever. Dead forever.

"Hey, c'mon homie," said Jesse.

Bruce couldn't see the jungle anymore. The whole thing had smeared; just a blur, a rainbow-colored smudge. Within it, his mother's smile. A tear spilled from each of his eyes, dribbled down each of his clean-shaven cheeks.

"Do you want a hug?" said Jesse.

And Bruce was through. He didn't need a hug. He snuffled; wiped his eyes. Cleared his throat. Gazed out at the party.

"That's fucking beautiful man," said Bruce after some time.

Jesse turned to look. "I know man."

Jesse paused.

"I don't see any viridescent headdresses though…"

"Oh, I do," said Bruce. "I see it all. I see glorious people of the night. Happy people. And not windows this time. Real, glorious people. Dancing in the water, in the jungle surrounding it. Partying in the space station in the hills."

"Seating areas like a wonderful pair of br—"

"Okay," said Bruce. "Whose house is this anyway?"

"Ha!" barked Jesse. "Wouldn't you like to know!"

41

"Dude! Whose fucking house are we at right now?" demanded Bruce.

"I'll tell you in a minute," assured Jesse, turning away. "But first we have a festival to get to!"

"Jesse," said Bruce. "Are you insane?"

"Night is young, motherfucker!" proclaimed Jesse.

Los Angeles, Washington D.C., Santa Fe
Nov 2017–Feb 2018

Vuiru Lake

Vuiru Lake

In the south of Ollu there is a lake encircled by towering soft cliffs. On certain mornings when the sun rises Vuiru Lake burns like gold, and the same happens on certain evenings when the sun falls. Every now and then, news spreads across Ollu of another wayward soul who has tried to reach the bottom of Vuiru Lake. The problem is that Vuiru Lake is bottomless. Every Ollite knows this. But it doesn't change anything. There will always be those for whom the beauty of Vuiru Lake is so mysterious, that in they will dive, and downward they will swim, never to return.

In a house by the lake lived a young woman named Vivian. She walked by the lake often, because it was one of the most beautiful parts of Ollu, overall a dirty and ugly city. It was a burning spring evening when, in the distance, she saw the stranger dive into the gold. His dark figure was gone; she'd nearly missed it. But Vivian was sure of what she'd seen. She sprinted to the spot where he'd disappeared and stripped off her clothes. Sure the man was trying to reach the bottom, she dove into the water.

Vivian came from a family of champion swimmers. The water's depth was terrifying, but she was determined to save the misguided man. Downward she swam, until she felt as though her head was imploding. When she opened her eyes, by the dying strands of gold she saw movement. Vivian lunged forward and pulled at the man's leg as hard as she could, but he kicked back at her, hell-bent on swimming down. With a final effort, Vivian wrapped her entire body around the man's torso. The man struggled... and relented. In her arms, briefly he looked at her. His face was covered in black hair and his eyes were striking and crazed.

Both were breathless. It was difficult to know which way was up; so together they swam toward the light. At the lake's surface they gasped for air, eventually coming to a stop on the bank.

"I was trying to touch the bottom," said the man.

"There is no bottom," replied Vivian. "Vuiru Lake is bottomless."

"I almost touched the bottom," said the man, shaking his dripping head. "I was so close."

Vivian watched as the stranger stood, gathering his clothes. He looked at her, and said, "But thank you for trying to save me." Vivian watched as he smiled and walked away.

One afternoon, at the party of a rich man, Vivian stood in a circle of six, listening to an older gentleman. Though the older gentleman spoke with great energy, Vivian had lost track of the topic, and was thrilled when she recognised the dark-haired man, who, through the people and the glinting wine-filled glasses, was smiling and waving at her. In return she beamed, and her small nose lifted, and her hair flashed. He moved to her, introducing himself. His name was Sebastian.

They walked down Dorachasu Boulevard later when the sky was dark enough for the golden streetlights to be on. Vivian and Sebastian spoke softly, yet with a kind of sureness; voices came from those at the tables; a pleasant wind moved through the leaves above. Turning into a street, they stopped speaking as the scene took them in. A warmth seemed to rise from the cobblestones, and Vivian and Sebastian each had the sense that they felt what the other felt. It was one of those rare moments when Ollu seemed like a beautiful city.

"Why did you try to save me?" asked Sebastian.

"Why did you try to touch the bottom of Vuiru Lake?" was Vivian's laughing reply.

"Because I couldn't help it," answered Sebastian.

"You must never try that again," said Vivian, shaking her head. "People die trying to touch the bottom of Vuiru Lake. The lake is bottomless."

Sebastian was silent. But he felt immensely grateful to Vivian; and Vivian knew this.

Again and again over the following weeks, Vivian and Sebastian met. In restaurants and cafés they spoke about themselves, until the day came when each began to speak about the other. Around them the green grass thickened, and the colourful flowers bloomed. The winds warmed and strengthened, and over their heads the waving trees swelled.

Whenever Vivian saw Sebastian in the distance she was struck by his stature; and when he was close she liked to watch him speak. He had such an odd way about him. In conversation, often Vivian found herself sure Sebastian had missed everything she'd said. But he'd prove her wrong, and at times would shock her with the precision of his memory.

Sebastian spoke often of the pain of existence, in both joking and serious contexts; but he told Vivian of how once he had loved life. With tears in his dark eyes he spoke about what he called the *'holes in his soul'*. He was like this the first time Vivian held his hand.

"I'm so happy I met you," said Sebastian that day.

For Sebastian, coming to Vivian was like coming home. The world for him was cold, and not a happy place. But Vivian—she was. Sebastian said that when Vivian smiled, he felt as though beautiful music echoed across the streets of Ollu. *'Music that will echo forever.'*

"I'm so happy I saved your life," said Vivian in reply.

And suddenly she felt cold inside, and shivered, and remembered how ugly Ollu was. And Vivian knew that she had not saved Sebastian's life.

They began to make love around the time summer arrived. As heat warmed the streets and the parks, and the light lasted into the nights, Vivian and Sebastian fell deeper and deeper into one another. Neither could remember being happier.

But Vivian was tormented by Sebastian's yellow-toothed smile.

"Never go near Vuiru Lake again," she beseeched him.

"Why not?" joked Sebastian; but he soon learned she was not laughing.

Every time Vivian and Sebastian met, together they flew through the warm skies of love. Vivian introduced Sebastian to her friends and her family; Sebastian did the same, though he had less of each. They attended performances and laughed the nights away. When they were able, they slept at one another's houses; but usually it was Sebastian's house, because Vivian's was close to the lake. Together they even travelled far away: to the quaint town of Eppia, and to the lush hills of Rannalum.

But every time they parted, Vivian fell. All around her the summer would grow cold, and unwillingly she would ruminate about what Sebastian was doing. Was he swimming? Was he trying to touch the bottom of Vuiru Lake? Vivian drove herself crazy this way. And then they would meet, and everything would be good once again.

Before they knew it, summer had passed, and the streets of Ollu were covered in dead leaves. And still the mercurial cycle continued. When she was with Sebastian the world was a good place. And when she was without him, the world was a terrible place, and Vivian would wonder whether she felt the way Sebastian felt always.

Vivian hated to be overbearing. But sometimes she was compelled to plead with him.

"Why are you so broken?" she asked, trembling in his arms one autumn evening.

"I'm not," he replied simply, running his fingers through her hair.

"Why would you want to touch the bottom of Vuiru Lake?" she whispered.

"It was a stupid mistake," answered Sebastian. "One I will never make again."

That night Vivian dreamt she was trying to save him. Down she swam into the gold water, down and down and down. He was down there, and she was a much stronger swimmer than he, so she knew she would find him eventually. But he was nowhere to be seen. She swam down forever…

And when the sun rose the next morning, Vivian floated dead upon Vuiru Lake, and all around her the water burned like golden fire.

Bucharest, Tirana, Mostar
Jul 2018

Cascading Light and Sexual Eternity

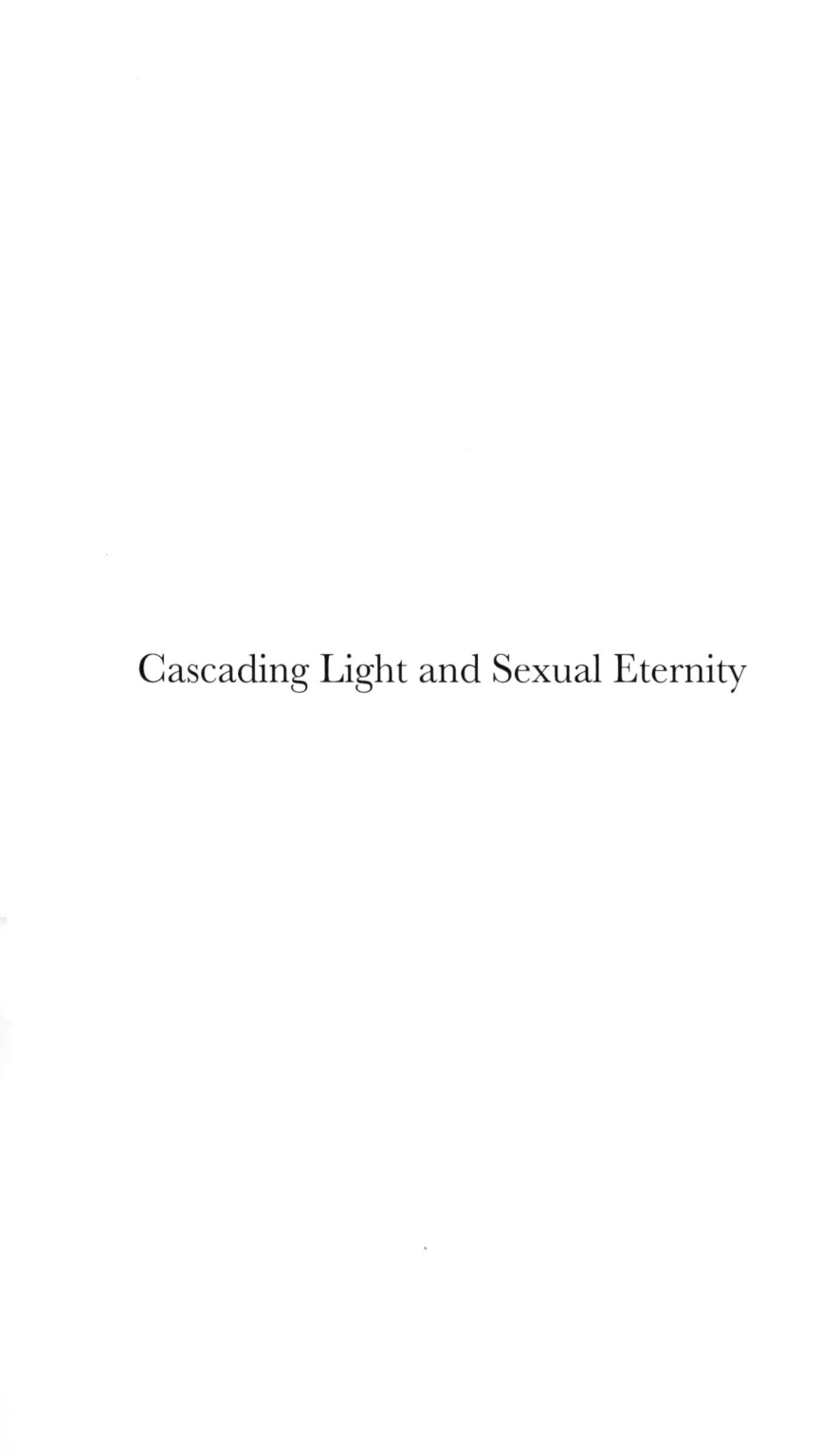

Joy for you and jouissance for she. Open upwards for endless white. Walk through white doors to find her access. Walk through white door after white door to open your mind and find what she's looking for. He's she and she's he because it's endless and the door to the next room is upon the pangolin but it's all okay and the people don't follow but she continues into further white doors to continue to seek out the pure joy that's for everyone.

You see, he's a man, and they're a person, and she's walking through white doors. She's sober. She hasn't taken any drugs, aside from food and water. Behind they're taking drugs and partying into the morning and blasting their minds and missing the purity that's simple joy.

"It's funny," she says.

Life's funny for everyone. Behind, inside, outside elsewhere they're boom-crashing between decorated walls, banging their heads, opening their minds by simultaneously closing their minds. And she was one of them—she'll always be one of them—but now she's she. She's free. She's…

"Rhondelle."

Visionary she opens the white door and inside there's an unfolding diverging fiery glare. Light bulges its eyes, heat flares its nostrils, fire tenses its jaw and flames flush its face. It opens out and crosses over and gentle Rhondelle feels her blood rise, she feels her skin sweat. Crackles and sniffles line the white walls as the divergent flames converge and open out and the glare intensifies—its eyes pop forth, its teeth unleash, it screams, and she charges through the crimson and fluorescent yellow to the white door as the glare explodes into an inferno, meaner, a goddamn firestorm of straight fury, and she's overwhelmed. Onward she flies like an aeroplane to its city which is jouissance exactly as Cixous knows it, toward the city of jouissance, toward. She opens the white door and feels her fingers melt at its handle.

Through white hallways, upward she falls, downward she climbs into the neverending effervescence of above, which appears as though in a dream before poor Rhondelle feels it all sink and her senses open out so that she's closed up for openness. It all makes impeccable nonsense as that's all we ever will ever have, just as decreasing, decreasing, sinking, darkening, opening forward eternally, as behind Max and Dervla and her friends and her enemies party on, bop to music, bounce to beat, sing out and across sideways their dear friend, she, uncaged and untouchable can beat the darkness that lies below which as we all know wins always and claims its victims for ravenous consumption and subsequent digestion. Below the hallway through which she glides, below down somewhere, she doesn't want to think on that hard-hitting manic drug-fuelled turpitude that charges all her friends and acquaintances and—

"Well not all of them."

True, not all of them but you know how it opens out and all crosses over in the end and sweeps through and across because freedom and repetition show her struggling now to keep on along the darkening hallway of the party she's left. In her pure open mind she's left the party but in her environment it's clear she hasn't—no, she must be lost, deep in the depths of the mansion hosting the party she'd attended and partied at and moved through so that she could be forward from all of it.

Presently she struggles—

"No!"

—as her clean closed mind tells her it's all okay but that of course it's not because it all opens out and the dark dark darkening threatens and attacks and howls with unrestrained laughter which she hears now, somewhere outside, Tide cleaning, distant muffled by walls which were white but which now are so fucking black it's sad.

Yet despairing she knows it's all ahead. All of it and everything else. She knows there's so much more, always more before she dies, which she's never feared, which she's always accepted, which she loves even.

"No."

She disagrees but agrees because you know, stepping forward still, somehow, never stopping, never stop—for within without she streams as nature blossoming and realises and upends herself as flowing knowledge that it was all always psychological construction streaks forth and she agrees and smiles. Theories of psychological construction suggesting her emotion lies always within her mind, emotions lie always within all of our minds, emotion is understood only in its context and is invented by us perhaps to serve practical purposes like moving on forward through the depths of the party and out and, you know, survival and things like that—showing emotion's complex and varied and exists innately yet only in our *minds* which are the be all and end all of what we call real but no!

Because reality exists independent of us, we are simply part of it, she knows this as for just a second she remembers her friends

Max and Dervla, remembering them, praying for them, knowing they'll be okay as she pushes them out of her mind to expel upward for the transcendent state representing freedom from linearities toward pure open mind that's joy for she and jouissance for you, and everything else and all the rest as it closes down and's ready for nothing. She's past the perc-and-molly-charged party, the coke and the acid-infused weed haze she thinks of no longer — she's past the fiery infernal stare of brutal rage and the endless slamming darkness that brings her down forever no longer. She seeks sexual enlightenment, complete and utter release as well as sheer unchaining from Freud's bullshit and Max's trash and the idiots and the dumbasses and the lovely boys she'll probably talk to again sometime but not soon probably never. This is all behind and she's sane as a rock as she walks through another nice white door to the people beyond.

"What—"

The guys turn around as Rhondelle notices their white butts pulse. Rapists.

"Get off her!"

"Ohh, ohh," goes the tall one as his latissimus dorsi undulates. "Shit."

A girl howls between the legs of the young men. Struggling to breathe, Rhondelle dives for the tall one's ankles.

"Oh shit!" he says as his semen hits the girl's torn mouth.

"Come with me!" wails Rhondelle and takes the girl below her limp arms.

"Damn," says the short rapist.

"Get out of here and never come back." Rhondelle's firm.

"Sorry, fuck, I'm sorry."

"Are you okay?"

The girl can only cry.

"Come with me."

Now she takes the girl, who clings to her, and spurns the stunned rapists. She walks the girl on her journey through further successive white doors.

The young girl shudders.

"Sorry?" Rhondelle leans closer.

"Where are you taking me?" the naked young girl shudders under Rhondelle's non-melted left hand.

"To the hospital."

"You saved me."

"No I didn't."

"But you saved me."

Rhondelle thinks of the rapists, all of the world's disgust propensity-eliciting degenerate rapists, who will never cease to rape but who must closer to the end of all time of course cease to rape, to hurt fellow humans simply for the sake of their orgasms. She knows the girl's right but she knows the girl's wrong and she answers:

"You're welcome."

She looks at her melted right hand but knows already it's fine and normal, for her mind's clear and she perceives correctly. She opens a dresser and finds jeans and a button-down shirt. Men's clothes, of course. They'll have to do.

"Put these on."

She looks at the defiled wailing girl, who takes a while before moving the mile with her saviour Rhondelle in the Uber to the hospital that's shut down at this hour. She'd thought the sky'd be lighter.

"I wanna go home," says the girl, eyes wet. She can't fully open her mouth.

Rhondelle realises how young the girl is. Softly she kisses her on the side of her face not covered in blood. Rhondelle cognises her hate for the men that would never be men that did what they did to the girl and doubtlessly to countlessly more.

She checks her phone. It's 3:25am.

"It's probably better if I just take you home."

Now the dim electric lights of the emergency building shoot past as Rhondelle and the girl take another Uber to the girl's home. It's small and dark, in an avenue full of houses that all look the same. The front door's white.

They walk through. Rhondelle stands in the black entranceway as the girl vanishes into the bathroom. So strange. But she has a job to do.

The girl emerges from the bathroom, clean, dressed in her own clothes, as though nothing'd happened to her — except that her lips are torn.

"Are your parents here?"

"Yes," whispers the girl. "Thanks for taking me home."

"I should tell your parents what happened."

"You don't need to do that."

"They need to know what happened to their daughter."

"I'll tell them tomorrow. Thanks for taking me home. I really mean it!"

In the dark house Rhondelle stands and stares. How can the girl's parents not know?

"They're asleep right now. I don't want to bother them."

"Tell them when they—"

"I will."

"Give me your number. I want you to text me tomorrow. Please?"

"Okay, sure."

The sighing girl tells her her number as Rhondelle types it into her phone.

"What's your name?"

"Britney."

Rhondelle types it and saves. And like that, she's through the white door, out in the cold, alone, wondering whether she'd done the right thing.

She's telling an Uber driver the mansion's address for her friends are still at the party. Her mind's clear because she doesn't drink, she doesn't smoke, she doesn't take drugs—she barely even takes caffeine. But tonight she's opening her mind, and things are a little crazy and'll probably continue so.

After thanking her driver, she walks through the giant white door of the mansion to find it quiet inside. She checks her phone. It's 5:11am.

"What the..."

She calls Dervla.

"Hey babe. Where are you?"

"We're downstairs. Where've you been?" Dervla's words come slowly.

"Oh, something happened. I need to tell you."

"We're just downstairs in the basement."

"I'll be there in a sec. Love you."

"Love you too Rhondelle."

She feels a warm flush as she remembers her friend.

Downstairs red lights are on. Friends and enemies lie around. Dervla's with ten others in a corner. Her dreads are out silver and she smiles when she sees Rhondelle.

"Where were you?" slurs Dervla.

"I've been everywhere. I walked in on someone being raped."

A few heads rotate before collapsing back onto chests and walls. Dervla's stays up.

"What?"

"Someone got raped, Dervla."

"Someone got raped?"

"Yes."

"I can't handle this," and Dervla's head falls back onto someone's shoulder.

Now Rhondelle heaves Dervla out of the pile of junkies.

"We're leaving this party. Where's Max?"

"Fuck. He already left. Why do you have to do this?"

"Someone was raped!"

"Someone was raped?"

She takes Dervla to the basement's white door but Dervla's turning to one of the junkies. They're joking about something and dry-heaving. Rhondelle waits patiently. Someone stares at

Rhondelle, mouth circular, eyes circular, eyebrows raised. Someone else turns the corners of their lips up at each end. Briefly Rhondelle smiles back, before asking:

"Ready to go, Dervla?"

"Um, yep."

They exit the basement and ascend several staircases, passing old paintings, then cavernous lounges filled with Art Deco furniture. She hears a deep growling from behind a wooden table. Turning, Rhondelle sees something alive behind there—it's so dark and nearly impossible to see, but she's sure. Quivering, she takes Dervla by the wrist and dashes to the house's exit. They're outside in the fresh air and it's lightening.

"Max is home right?"

"Max?" mumbles Dervla. "He's gone."

"Where is he?"

"I don't fucking know."

"Dervla! Is he safe?"

"…yeah."

"Are you sure?"

"Max is all good."

Rhondelle closes her eyes and inhales the morning air. She exhales, and opens her eyes.

"Let's go home."

"That was such a good party."

"I mean, someone got raped there Dervla."

"Someone got raped there?!"

"Jeez. Yes."

"That's bad," says Dervla.

"And I saw a mean face, and I think I got lost, and I saw a monster behind a table."

"Can I crash at yours?"

Rhondelle sighs.

"Sure."

They're in an Uber. They're driving to Rhondelle's apartment. Beat but gentle and psychologically open forever, she unlocks the front door which's white and behind Dervla collapses silver onto the sofa.

"Love you Rhondelle."

"You gotta stop taking that stuff."

"I will. Love you."

"Love you too. Goodnight."

She checks the front door's locked. She checks again. Satisfied, she takes the thin blanket and places it over Dervla's body. She turns on the apartment heating. She moves to the shower. She washes, hair dry safely under her patterned cap. She tastes morning and her mind's collapsing in the worst possible way. She thinks of the girl and, after drying, makes a reminder on her phone for 6pm tomorrow: "Text the girl". She puts on her pyjamas. She rolls into bed and feels so warm as tears fill her eyes. She opens her mind and falls asleep.

And so she's walking through white doors toward the pure joy in all things. She's falling down and her chest's heavy and perfect and sleep sleep sleep pulls her down into sad euphoria. It's all opening out and closing in and the white door takes Rhondelle forth into floating dreams that let go and carry her sexually into something better than the horrible things she'd seen earlier that night-day in her real life. Another white door takes her to a highly decorated refrigerator in the rich house she'd left and she jerks awake.

"Not there."

She tastes morning in her mouth and trembles into a lower and forthcoming wave of sleep. Waves and waves and sea and sea wash over her but it's okay because she can breathe underwater—she thinks not at all but always in some way and her consciousness ceases to exist because she's asleep but not really because she's alive. Her circadian rhythm takes its toll and she recycles and replenishes her tortured torturous mind without having to do a thing but of course she's doing it all as it's she, Rhondelle the mild, and her mind splits open underwater so that flowing, sinking, swimming down and up and breathing at the surface and diving down again toward relaxed wakefulness and slow eye movement and the theta wave and deeper down below the waves into the harder waters where her eyes are still and her sleep spindles and K-complexes abound and taking a deep breath for in her dream she breathes water dives deeper down again into deep sleep delta waves and clarity of sense, of surrounding, of being, of existing within the ocean of her dream. There's a white door at the bottom of the ocean so she swims for it, down towards the door, and but she remembers she can't breathe underwater and swims harder and harder for the door but it's so far away and her air runs out and out and out and her eyes stream. She swims on. Down and down. Harder and harder, pushing, forcing, she reaches out and the door's at her hand and she's through the last white door.

And there's free air and she ascends a perfect white staircase and up there there's whiteness. Pure whiteness. Not the white that's whiter than light, but the white that's limitlessly lighter than white and inexpressibly whiter than white. Her mind's open and jouissance is above and tracking trekking surely in she sees shimmering. It's a waterfall but it's lighter, brighter. It's all of it and everything else and of course it still crosses over and wins and loses and breaks open upon the solid foundation upon which it's built — and that's it so she connects with it and knows it's Dervla and the poor girl and flowing, rolling, wet like deliquescent hydrogen hydrogen and oxygen liquid but shining like our old and faithful faultless and unwaveringly chemically and physically sustaining star, which continuing and perpetually providing crosses over as all else and'll be there always forever even when long after we're dead it'll die yet continue on for everything dies which is the only way things live so that eternity's the only thing real, the cascading light upends for it's already upended and there's no direction down here or anywhere, only eternity, and falls agreeing with its essence as a waterfall but *rises* upholding its process of evaporation and its very existence as being a part of all of it and everything else, as it connects with her as human to human and rises like joy and laughs and sprouts up as water springs to its gravitational centre which is down, but which, of course, is up on the opposite side of the globe, and glitters, winking, twinkling. The cascading light that is all people and all things including most of all Dervla, the rape victim, and she, flips out cracks through and takes her onward and up to jouissance and joy and the furtherance and skywardness of her dream.

The sweet singing of the cascading light and sexual eternity continues to be nothing less than hilarious and she laughs calmly and meekly as she laughs and it all makes plentiful sense up here in the caverns of low-voltage desynchronised brain waves abundance of acetylcholine atonia and suspension of homeostasis just as it does always and forever in the regular day-to-day human experience anyway for her mind's pure and open always and unchangingly for it all crosses out and flips across and expresses and's real. And it all comes she feels unstoppable from a bloom, from the opening calyx and unspeakably polychromous blooming corolla of a lotus whose wonderful electromagnetic radiation's moved through and on and always by undying brilliant ceaseless wave function collapse magic from the place the horror she'd witnessed had wanted to come from as the writer writes liquid and you read solid and this continues on into forever forever and she simply laughs because she knows Dervla one day will quit heroin and the young girl with her bloodied face sullied by her rapist's cum will tell her parents what happened to her and will live a tarnished tattered life that will in the end of all things be okay and joyous and laughable and light just as in the end of all things all of our lives will love everything and be okay and joyous and laughable and lighter than the cascading light and sexual eternity that carries Rhondelle into infinity and beyond. And her cognition's asleep and her development's developed and her problems destroy her and hold her back and keep her sick but'll be treated and ultimately cured and her emotions are happy and her trait openness is stifled and closed yet open forever because she's totally sober as she's essentially always been for she's a sweet young woman untouched by any of that, of course she is, every day is a new day and tomorrow is another day and it's never black and white but of course she's as sober and everything-loving and clear-headed as anyone can be in her dream and outside it and it's all what it is. And we all take drugs and of course that's untrue yet true yet totally untrue yet Rhondelle's always totally drugless, that's her nature, that's her baseline, that's her. And the light cascades and the eternity has sex and it's all love, beauty, and most of all, jouissance for she and joy for all of you and a bit of a giggle.

"Haha."

And lying in her bed she sleep-laughs.

Melbourne
Nov 2019

Viral

Chapter 1

"The world's most liveable city."

A French tourist said those words and a small figure on a nearby stone ledge laughed. The French tourists pointed their iPhone 11s at the graffiti-covered laneway wall. They may as well have pointed handguns at a rope-bound group of hostages. They were taking photos of someone's tag, scribbled in white over someone else's tag, yellow, which obscured ten more tags of various colours below. This was beautiful Melbourne street art, soon to become Instagram-Famous.

The small figure who had laughed was dressed in black. He sat on the ledge with his knees pointing up. His jeans were black yet were visibly filthy. His t-shirt hadn't always been black. His boots were tattered and stained. He held a grubby notebook with a black pen through the binder in his right hand. He held a smoking self-rolled cigarette between the pointer and middle fingers of his left hand. His fingernails resembled dried mustard. His face suggested he was Chinese. His face was tanned and scarred at the lips and expressed joyless laughter and not much else. His face did not express nausea. He felt nauseous.

The French tourists jumped when a yell came down the alleyway.

"What's goin' on Alan you cunt?"

A ragged, bearded man lurched toward them. The French woman bent to pick up her giant pink iPhone 11, which in her fright she had dropped in the sewage. Her French man watched Alan, who made nothing in the way of a response to the bearded man, instead continuing to sit on the ledge and to express joyless laughter.

"Nice phone!" screamed the hairy old man at the woman. His voice was hoarse and the tourists could already smell him. The smell was of garbage and urine.

The tourists backed away and the old man shouted. Slowly Alan lifted his left hand to drag from his cigarette. He watched people spill into the alleyway behind the old man. Young guys, white, dressed to kill. 12, 13, 14 of them. Alan looked to his left and saw the French tourists fleeing around the corner and out of sight. The hairy man stood shouting. Alan looked to his right and saw, beyond the rich white boys, several others stalking into the alleyway. A huge bald brute with green tattoos around his dark eyes. A wiry First Australian man limping on a bad left leg. A red-hot young rager known to every shop-owner on Swanston Street. A lumbering woman whose white belly cascaded to her knees. A tiny screaming rat-faced meth addict. A junkie whose face was never visible below his soiled red cap.

Alan stood to follow the tourists but the hairy man, Phillip, was having a moment. "...the reconciliation and the gentrification...," Phillip was saying. Then Phillip said something else but Alan failed to hear it because the white boys were hollering about the upcoming footy season. Alan stood back against the greasy wall to let them pass. The rat-faced meth-head had seen Alan and was clamouring for his attention.

Alan looked to his left and saw three more tourists entering the alleyway. Alan could tell they were Malaysian. Two small women and one man, all dressed to enjoy a wonderful summer evening in Melbourne. Alan cringed. Why had so many people come here all at the same time?

The meth-head, Andy, was sprinting through the white boys toward Alan. Alan gave Andy a tight smile. Andy shot his forearm around Alan's neck and patted him hard on the stomach. Alan wretched and smiled. Everything stunk. Then one of the Malaysian tourists squealed. Alan inhaled sharply and looked across at her. She was squealing up at one of the white boys.

"You gonna act racist to me? We are just trying to enjoy. You gonna act tough in front your friends?"

Alan placed his notebook carefully on the stone ledge and dropped his cigarette in the sewage. The rich boys were forming a ring around the three tourists. Alan turned to beckon the meth-head and got through the ring with ease. The tiny Malaysian woman was screaming and stamping her foot and the Malaysian man's shouting red face was within licking distance of the blondest white boy's face. The blonde boy's taller friend pushed the Malaysian man in the chest and it was as though a bomb went off. Alan pounced on the pusher and heaved his radius back into the guy's throat, and the two of them fell backwards onto another of the rich boys. Someone got Alan hard in the right eye before they hit the ground. The huge bald man's shouts were like a Rottweiler's barks and as usual the Swanston-Street-famous rager was on Level 10. Those two could take down four of the rich white boys. Andy the meth-head had his switchblade in his rotting hand and was facing off with a freckled red-head. Half of the white boys had retreated to the mouth of the alley. The Malaysian woman was still squealing and Alan kept her in his line of sight because it was his duty to protect the three tourists. The slightly-less-short second Malaysian woman was cowering in a corner and the taller Malaysian man was hidden in a writhing mass of bodies. Into this mass the corpulent white woman dived. A white boy smashed Alan in the stomach and all of his breath disappeared. Yet somehow in his breathlessness his mind awoke. All of a sudden he saw clearly. He watched as Emanuel, the face-tattooed giant, whipped his folded chain across his opponent's face, which snapped to the side. He watched as two sweating white guys stomped Andy's rat-body and three more of their mates saw this and joined in. Alan saw one of the cowards who'd retreated to the alley's mouth approach the squealing Malaysian woman from behind. He saw the coward cover the lady's mouth with his white hand and he saw him throw her to the side. Alan shot to the boy like a bullet and with everything he had, swung a right hook into the boy's head. The entire line of cowards saw this; none did anything more than yell. The boy crashed onto an utterly gorgeous mural depicting a demented alien monkey with grossly oversized fangs. Alan gently lifted the small woman to her feet, not noticing the pain in his right hand. The woman sobbed and squealed so hard Alan couldn't tell if she was actually aware of his presence. Alan sought the Malaysian man but perceived only a mess of human bodies. Andy the meth-head lay crumpled in blood. Phillip was on the ledge taking care of one of the notebooks Alan had forbidden him to open; Philip cried into his beard. Beside Phillip the First Australian sat shaking his head. The red-headed boy's face was screwed up, and he supported himself with one hand clutching a dank windowsill, the other hand at the stab-wound in his stomach. Alan saw a mess of human but was unable to distinguish the Malaysian man. Instead he saw giant Emanuel spinning his twice-folded steel chain, preparing to whip another white boy across the face. But this white boy had a strange look in his blue eyes. Alan could not tell what that look meant. But he could tell one thing. This white boy was not a real fighter. Alan tried to yell but only wretched again. Somehow he had forgotten his nausea. Alan spat into the sewage. He tried again.

"Manny."

The spinning chain slowed. The chain drooped. Emanuel turned.

Alan shook his head.

Emanuel looked back at Alan like he was going to kill someone. The green tattoos squirmed around his eyes. The eyes exuded hate. Emanuel raised his chain.

"Don't," Alan said.

Emanuel swore and threw his chain at the red-head, who collapsed.

The rich boy who was not a real fighter still had the same look in his bright blue eyes. But now those eyes were directed at Alan's. This white boy smiled.

Immediately Alan looked down into the corner and vomited. When he had finished vomiting, he spat several times, and looked again at the mess. At last he saw the Malaysian man lying face-down among three of the rich white boys. Alan relaxed, and as soon as he did, the pain in his eye and his stomach came on. Alan wretched again, but did not vomit. He stepped over the bodies to the Malaysian man. He bent, and rolled the man onto his back.

The man's face was covered in blood and his eyes were closed. His nose was the wrong shape and his summer shirt would never be white again. But he breathed steadily. Alan slid his arm under the Malaysian man's neck and lifted him into a sitting position. The Malaysian woman was still sobbing but was no longer squealing, and she had hopped over the bodies and was helping Alan to support her companion.

"Are you alright?" Alan asked her.

The sobbing woman seemed not to hear him. She was trying to lift her companion to his feet but she would never achieve this by herself. Alan and the woman slowly lifted the unconscious man out of the pile of human. Alan had the man's upper body and the woman had her companion's feet. They co-ordinated to the extent that they were able to sit the unconscious man upright against the alleyway wall next to the third tourist, who was phoning an ambulance, or similar. Alan's phone didn't work anyway. Alan stepped through the bodies to the ledge where bearded Phillip held out his hand. Alan shook the hand. Philip then passed Alan his deteriorating black notebook. Alan took it and nodded. He stepped once more over the bodies. He walked past the rich cowards who had chosen to stand back and watch their friends get bashed. These cowards would become businessmen, investors, CEOs. Alan glanced over his shoulder and noticed that the boy with the blue eyes was still watching him. Alan shivered and left the laneway.

Chapter 2

It was summertime in Melbourne and everyone knew it. In a beer garden in the central business district drinkers of all types flickered around like lights. Greasy-haired young women laughed in tube tops. Oil-faced fellas jostled in shorts and flip-flops. Older ladies watched. Older guys smoked. The beer was cold and the mood was good.

But the summer had been a tragic one. The year was 2020. Bushfires had destroyed the states of Victoria and New South Wales, 18 million hectares of Australian land in total. 3 billion animals had been affected and at least 30 people had been killed. No one was quite sure whether or not the fires had ended. These people were at this beer garden built into the side of some laneway for a variety of reasons. Some aimed to socialise. Others had been forced here by friends. Some aimed to get drunk. Others did not drink. Some were present for The Lights, the rock band who were scheduled to take the stage at 9:00pm. Unbeknownst to many, this was a bushfire relief concert. All proceeds from the night's ticket sales and bar takings would support the national effort to rebuild and to rehabilitate. Hanging in the air was the vague promise that, far away, countless koalas were grateful.

But it was only 6:15pm and someone stood on the stage, large dark patches under the arms of his light pink shirt, tapping the microphone with his fingernail. Nobody noticed this useless man, other than an obese middle-aged loner in a corner, a quiet teenager who found her surroundings more interesting than her drunk boyfriend, and a young fella with soft blonde hair and bright blue eyes.

The latter had entered the laneway beer garden as part of a pack. Leaning a forearm on the wooden corner of the bar, the young man with blue eyes had watched the sound man with the light pink shirt scuttle onto the stage, look around with beetle eyes, scuttle off the stage, stand at the opposite end of the bar, consider buying a drink, decide against buying a drink, scuttle back on to the stage, and finally, begin to tap the microphone with his fingernail. Then one of the boys in the pack had declared the venue *shit* and the boy with the blue eyes had begun a commentary on the useless sound guy in order to cheer up his friend. It worked. The twinkles in the azure eyes brought summertime to the friend's face.

"*Check one two.*"

"*Testing*, uh, *testing.*"

"*Seeeew* could I get a bit more of those highs? Thank you sir. *Seeeewup.*"

"Ah *ahhh* uhuh. Get that high note. *Aaahhhh* that's it."

The boy with the blue eyes laughed like a dingo, and his soft fringe bounced. His name was Luke.

"Mate get on the stage," another friend in a yellow-and-pink Hawaiian shirt said.

"There's a stage there," a third friend said, nodding at the microphone-tapper.

"Don't tempt me," Luke said. Suddenly he stood on his toes and appeared confused. Their boy Max was roaring about another friend, Thornton, who was at another bar. Max's large shoulders were swinging around towards the beer garden's exit.

"Alrighty then," the man in the yellow-and-pink Hawaiian shirt said. He shrugged at Luke. The entire group left the beer garden. They pushed down the bricky laneway.

"Owen mate you don't even know what's coming. I'm gonna be the best stand-up comedian in Australia. No fucking joke mate. I'm gonna be the funniest guy since Robin Williams. Do you believe in reincarnation? Nah of course you don't mate. I'm Robin Williams reincarnate, mate. You better believe it. What, you think an everlasting soul like Robin Williams's everlasting soul just leaves the Earth and never comes back? Is that how you think it works? I'm the funniest cunt you've ever met."

The guy in the Hawaiian shirt, Owen, was not listening. But a scrawny red-head with freckles said, "Like, I agree you're funny..." and then winced and clutched at the still-healing stab-wound in his stomach. Luke waited patiently for the red-head to continue. "You're funny. But first of all. Robin Williams died in like 2014. Even if you..." The red-head paused to breathe and wince. "Even if you act like it mate, you're not six years old. So how could you be... Robin Williams reincarnate?"

"You're right mate, it was 2014 when we lost that son of a God. And yeah, I was born all the way before that in 1997, even if I *have* got the maturity of your parents. But 2014 was the year I *became* a comedian. So I'm Robin Williams."

"And that's the thing," the red-head panted. "That's the second thing. I agree you're funny. But how... how can you talk like all that if you've never actually performed?"

Luke had expected the question. The red-head, Nick, was hobbling badly and falling behind the group, who were on their way to whichever bar Max's friend was at. Luke fell behind with Nick.

"Oh, I'll perform soon," Luke said. "I just don't think anyone's really in a laughing mood at the moment. Everyone's gotten real serious since the fires, you know?"

"You're..." Nick inhaled in pain. "You're not really... sensitive, are you?"

This comment filled Luke with sudden rage. Not sensitive? There wasn't a chance in hell Luke cared less about the victims of the fires than Nick did. In fact, the chance was slim that Luke cared less about the victims of the fires than any one of the boys who hulked in front of them in the summer-packed street. But Luke just said, "Oh, you're so *sensitive*," in an effeminate voice, making the *s* consonants whistle. Nick chuckled. Now Max's shoulders were entering the same dark doorway Luke had watched the shoulders enter this time last week. In single file the boys raced up the dark staircase within, headed for the same rooftop bar they had all gone to every week for the last five years. Luke repressed a sigh. He sought change. At the top of the stairs, the sun blazed, there were three times as many people as there had been in the laneway beer garden, and all were young. Max and his mate David Thornton hugged like bears. Two young brunettes approached Luke, who kissed and hugged them happily. The one with the black handbag over her shoulder was Dana; the one with golden tips was Kate. Luke had about eight pints of Carlton Draught. And somehow, by the time it was dark, they had all ended up back at that beer garden in the alleyway. A huge neon sign bore the shining words *The Lights*. Max's shoulders had said something about their mate Vince who was playing a set that night.

"When did Vince become a rock star?" Luke slurred, two metres from the band's bass player, sweating bodies pressed against him from all sides.

"That's not Vince," Max's shoulders declared. "Vince is playing later."

"Dude what are you talking about?" Will's turned mug demanded. "Vince is a DJ."

"Oh, no shit," Luke said. "Then what the fuck is this?"

"Some shit band."

Indeed, this was some shit band. The bass player was skinny and unmoving, with a mop of terrible brown hair on his solemn head. The bass player had no stage presence. In the centre of the stage was a wailing singer, a prima donna, feminine and buoyant. He looked a little different to the rest of his band. Luke could tell he was of mixed race. There was a lead guitarist at the far end of the stage, and with a jolt Luke realised that he knew this clown. His name was Louis. Years ago, Louis had gone to a private school whose circles ran adjacent to Luke's. Sometimes these circles overlapped. Louis had played footy against Luke's schoolmates countless times, was currently shirtless, and was absolutely obsessed with himself. Every now and then, Louis would extend a foot forward, turn his stupid guitar vertical, and play what Luke guessed was called a *solo*. Luke did not like Louis. Behind these three men sat a thick-limbed drummer, exerting huge effort toward his stick-swinging and drum-hitting, perspiring under the neon sign shimmering *The Lights*. The entire band looked like they had gone to private schools like Luke's. Luke did not have any interest in bands. But his guess was that a good band did not tend to be born of privilege. This was a band born of privilege. Luke was drunk and was only speculating. Regardless, this was a terrible band.

Which didn't make sense because there were two hundred people sweating in this godforsaken beer garden and Luke's pack were the only ones not enjoying themselves. Max's shoulders bellowed insults at the band. Thornton cupped his hands around his mouth and called the drummer *fat cunt* and Louis the guitarist *little bitch*. But the band must have been deaf. The singer jerked his tattooed arms up and down, like a handicapped woman, and all the real women in the crowd wooed and whistled. Luke looked across at them. A row of about six stood doe-eyed, transfixed by this disabled mixed-race singer. In front of these women were more women, drunk and high out of their minds, their eyes closed, dancing. Luke froze. One of these girls was his younger sister, Bailey. She was wearing mauve, her bare arms were in the air, and she swayed blindly, drawing unwanted attention to herself. Luke watched in horror as the singer of The Lights extended a tattooed, reedy forearm toward Bailey, who accepted the singer's hand and jumped up and down. The singer was bending forward to kiss Bailey's hand. Luke spun around and wriggled to the bar.

A Chinese-Malaysian man was in the back corner of the beer garden with a black eye and a decaying notebook. Alan sat at a table atop a crate-like structure of wooden planks, raised above the crowd. He had already been at this beer garden for four hours, drinking at the rate of one pint of Furphy per hour (all he could afford, and all he needed). Drinking the first pint, something had lifted in Alan, and beneath the table he had written a poem in his notebook. Then the first band, Rolling On Square Wheels, had taken the stage, Alan had started on his second pint, and it had all gone downhill from there. Alan had not paid for a ticket. He had not known there would be bands. Rolling on Square Wheels played something like avant-garde post-punk harsh-noise rock music, and though he had sincerely tried, Alan had not been able to enjoy it. The second band had been called Juicy Hippo Magic and were even worse than the first. But by this time, the beer garden's patrons had begun to repeat a certain phrase. *The Lights*. Something in the way this phrase was said—whispered at first, pronounced by the first support act with admiration and by the second with respect, this phrase *The Lights* finally filling out every lull and called out across the densifying crowd—this had kept Alan present in the beer garden. By night, the air was cool and the venue was lit by neon, and The Lights had shimmied onto the stage, and the beer garden had roared. But The Lights had disappointed Alan. They sounded like any other band. They could play well. But sitting above the crowd, Alan thought that he may as well have listened to the Red Hot Chili Peppers on Spotify. The Lights were just a copy.

Having finished four pints of Furphy, at last Alan stood to leave. But he watched a glass of beer arc over the front row and explode into the guitarist's towering amplifier. The shirtless guitarist unslung his instrument, placed it carefully on its stand, and hurled himself into the audience like a missile. The music had stopped mid-song and people were screaming. Alan stared at the guitarist. He was single-handedly brawling with ten guys in the audience, and as Alan stared, he recognised several of the guys. They were the idiots from the alleyway.

"Fellas, fellas, this is a charity concert," the singer of The Lights said into the microphone. The crowd were dispersing and shaking their heads. Some were crying.

"Fuck your band!" a douchebag in a yellow-and-pink Hawaiian shirt screeched. The douchebag watched several of his mates take down the guitarist, who was on his knees.

Then a white girl stepped onto the stage. She wore blocky mauve heels, a white mini skirt, and a mauve blouse with nothing underneath it. The singer, a half-Asian hipster with intricate tattoos on his bare arms, had led the woman onto the stage by the hand. She said into the microphone: "Boys, we're here to support bushfire relief. You've been acting like children the entire night. We're not here to punch on. We're here to support bushfire relief."

"Fuck the koalas!"

But the young woman's words had taken an effect. She seemed to be a friend of the idiots from the alleyway. Alan felt sorry for her; he almost liked her. The rich boys sheepishly reassembled and backed off, revealing the shirtless guitarist. He was crouched on the concrete with his arms over his head. The girl in the blouse jumped off the stage and the singer of The Lights followed her.

Alan escaped to the alleyway, which was packed in the wake of the commotion. Most of these people had never witnessed a fight. Alan tried to make his way through a group of women with mascara down their cheeks like black lightning. But it was impossible. Alan turned to leave in the opposite direction. Patrons sprinted through the gaps between other patrons. Alan jogged after them. He just wanted to be away from this beer garden. But now he was in some kind of makeshift backstage area, no less populated than the alley. The behemoth drummer stared into the soul of his shirtless bandmate, who was slumped against a stack of wood slabs.

"We're halfway through a set man. There are people waiting out there."

"He just had the shit beat out of him Hunter, give him a break."

"I can't play because my amp's shorted," the guitarist gasped, and dark blood spilled from his mouth and ran down his chin. "Unless we can find another amp... it's a night."

The woman in the mauve blouse and heels stood with her arms crossed. Her face was deadly serious. Beside her were three bulky white guys. One of them looked at Alan.

"This guy saved my life the other day," the guy said, and Alan experienced a sudden onset of acute nausea as he recognised the bright blue eyes.

"There's only one life-saver here," the woman in mauve muttered.

Alan pretended not to hear and walked where he saw space. But the boy with the blue eyes grabbed Alan's elbow and Alan stopped.

"What's your name, man?" the boy asked.

Alan looked at the concrete.

"Alan."

"Well, Alan, man. Sorry to bother you. But I recognised you from the other day and I wanted to introduce myself."

Suddenly a freezing breeze blew through the space. Suddenly it was not summertime. Three men suddenly felt infinitely sad. And three men simultaneously experienced the same thing: in that infinite sadness, a deep joy.

"I'm Luke."

"Hi."

"Hi. I'm Luke. Nice to meet you. I wanted to thank you for stopping your friend from hurting me the other day. He was ready to kill me with that chain thing."

"No worries," Alan said.

Alan was unsure where to look. So he looked up at the woman in mauve, who was already looking down at Alan.

"Hi, I'm Bailey. I'm Luke's sister."

"Hi, hi."

"And Bailey's the heroine of the night, and the most beautiful woman I've ever seen," said the hipster singer of The Lights, wheeling around from his bashed guitarist toward Alan. His tattooed hands were clasped together and he wore a smile on his face.

"I—I saw your show," Alan said. "That was good music. I—"

"You're too kind!" the singer exclaimed effeminately. "Oh, thank you, thank you! But next time you'll have to come and watch our full show. This one was cut short, unfortunately…"

"Yeah, cut short. It's a pity."

"I think it's a night," the bleeding and shirtless guitarist wheezed, sucking a cigarette. Hunter, the band's giant drummer, held his colossal arms to the sides and stared at the stars.

"Dude, Louis is right," the singer said to Hunter. "He doesn't have an amp."

"I'm just sad for the bushfire victims," Bailey sighed.

"Look, you did the right thing, Bailey. We'll organise another gig. Like, everyone's *trying* to give as much money as possible to the bushfire appeal. People will come." The singer was earnest, and Bailey seemed to trust him. "Sorry," the singer said to Luke. "Have we met?"

"No. I'm Luke. I'm Bailey's brother."

"Ohhh you're—of course you are! It's an absolute pleasure to meet you my friend. I'm Mark."

"You're a bitch-ass, Mark, and your band sucks," Luke said.

The backstage area went silent. The silence lasted for far too long.

"He's joking," panted Nick, the scrawny red-head, who had suddenly appeared out of nowhere. "I promise you, he's joking."

Luke grinned.

The singer burst out laughing. The sound was like that of a magpie.

"He is right though," Alan murmured. "Your band is not very good."

Mark the singer stopped laughing. Luke's dingo laugh replaced it.

"Is it just me?" Bailey said. "Or is this the beginning of something beautiful?"

Chapter 3

"I'm a comedian."

No one laughed. For Luke said the words with glazed eyes, with sad downturned lips, with a voice that was so flat you could drop a football on it and the football would never roll. Luke told the others he was a comedian the way Neville Chamberlain told the United Kingdom they were at war with Germany. Luke declared himself a comedian, and Mark and Alan got the creeps, and felt chills down their spines.

"I'm a musician."

Mark's words had a different effect. He pouted slightly, his moustache thin, his face effeminate. Bailey hummed in warm agreement. Alan believed Mark. Luke withdrew, the way a clam withdraws into its shell.

"I rock," Mark pouted.

"You suck," Luke said.

"And you must be a writer," Mark pouted to Alan.

Alan did not respond to Mark's comment. He only lifted his mustard-nails to drag from his grey cigarette. Strange, cold wind blew through the Southbank outdoor bar, though it was late February and should have been sweltering. Mark nodded.

"He's a fighter," Nick the red-head said.

"Shut up," Luke said.

"For real though. I saw him. His friend knifed me in the stomach, and I was bleeding everywhere, and I saw him knock out James Piper. He's fucking ruthless."

Alan shrugged. He sipped his Furphy.

Mark sipped at his Tallboy & Moose. "You *are* a fighter."

"Leave him alone," Bailey said.

"No, it's okay," Alan smiled.

Mark sucked his cigarette from a delicately-tattooed hand with a coruscating ring adorning the pinkie. He peered at Alan through a window of smoke. "You're a fighter and you're a writer."

"Why do you keep saying he's a writer?" Nick said.

"I can tell."

"He can *just tell*," Luke said.

"I can tell. He's all darkness. Darkness and beauty. He doesn't talk. He's too nice to talk. He sees the beauty and the darkness of the world and he writes about it. He feels more than, like, me, or you, or that guy over on that table, you know? He feels so much. He's more intelligent than, like, the smartest scientist. Because... he *feels*. Yeah. And he writes about it." Mark nodded in agreement with himself.

"He also carries a fucking notebook at all times," Luke added.

"That too."

"I'm so with you though," Bailey said to Mark. "Sorry, Alan, I know we're making you uncomfortable."

"No, I don't mind," Alan said.

"What do you write about?" Nick queried, ogling Alan's dark notebook.

Everyone watched Alan.

"Oh, you know," Alan said. "This and that."

Nick opened his mouth, but Bailey gave him a look.

"I write poetry," Alan said, and smoked.

"*Can I read some?*" Nick shouted.

Luke groaned. A few heads turned at another table.

"Oh, no, I don't think so," Alan smiled.

Bailey brimmed with excitement. Here were three guys who were so extremely different from one another. Yet Bailey sensed something between them. It was clear to her that the table's fifth member, snivelling, insipid Nick, did not belong on the same level. Bailey loved her brother, Luke; she always had. Luke was unique. His brilliance was recognised by so few. Luke spent his weekends crewing with his boys, all of whom Bailey loved, but none of whom saw in her brother what she saw. This was a giant shame. Yet here, now, were these *other* two! Oh, Mark. Bailey had fallen in love with Marcus Tze as soon as she had heard his voice on Spotify. Mark had crooned to her via her iPhone 10's tiny speaker, the lead vocalist on a trending Spotify track with a million hits, and Bailey had gone to see The Lights play at Falls Festival over the New Year. A dark figure on the distant stage, Mark had appeared to her, clear in the centre of the waving effect of the drugs she'd ingested. In that moment, Bailey had decided in advance to pursue this man. She heard rumours; that Mark was a womaniser; that he was extremely close with his mother, whose name was Ella; that his older brother was estranged from the broken family. Bailey did not know if any of this was true. She did not really care. At this time, the bushfire crisis had garnered international attention, and Bailey had given hundreds of dollars to the Red Cross appeal. When she had received a Facebook invitation to The Lights' bushfire relief concert, she had not thought twice about it. There, she had finally met him. He was so kind. His heart, right there on the edge of his sleeve, was so true. On the same night, backstage with him, her watchful brother nearby, Bailey had met Alan. And Bailey had liked Alan, too, though she didn't yet feel that she understood him.

Bailey knew only one thing.

All three of these young men would become famous.

They were talking about the 'coronavirus'; someone in Italy had contracted it and died. *"It's one person coming in from China,"* Luke was saying in a perfect imitation of Donald Trump. *"We have it totally under control."*

"Dude, do Trump," Nick shouted suddenly. "Show Mark—"

"He's doing it, Nick," Bailey said.

"Dude, Mark, I'm telling you I saw him do the best fucking Trump imitation. He's got it down. Luke, show him—Mark, I'm telling you. I saw it the other day. We're in the midst of a fucking genius."

Indeed, like fuel the redhead's adulations had caused something in Luke. Suddenly the comedy became apparent in the comedian. Luke's blue eyes were cocked, the right slightly narrower. His lower lip jutted out. The way his hands moved... everything was exactly right, everything was exactly Donald Trump, President of the United States.

Mark's phone was a battered iPhone 7 with a caramel-coloured leather case. Nick grabbed it off the wooden table and swiped its cracked screen from right to left. The look in the redhead's eyes was hysterical.

"What are you doing?" Mark demanded.

"For my Instagram Story. My phone's out of battery." Oblivious to potential objection, Nick began to use Mark's phone to film Luke's Trump impression.

"*...But I have great respect, admiration. And I cherish women! Hillary Clinton said, 'You shouldn't cherish women.' I said, 'I do cherish women! I love women!' My mother was like the greatest woman I've ever met!...*" Luke was undeniable. Nick and Bailey cackled. Alan smiled silently, smoking and nodding. People at other tables watched and laughed. And Mark, like everyone else, was transfixed. Yet Mark's face contorted. His mouth drew backward. His long-lashed eyes expanded like lasers. This was not mirth upon Mark's face. This was horror.

Mark retrieved his iPhone 7 from the redhead's gummy fingers. He hit the large red circle at the bottom of the screen. The video stopped.

"*Oi!*" Nick screamed.

"It's long enough," Mark said. "It's just for your Story, right?"

The table was quiet. Luke had stopped; Mark had killed the vibe.

"Send it to me," Nick whined. "For my Stor—"

"Hey, I know you!" came a sudden shout. Sitting at a slightly shorter table behind Mark was the remainder of Mark's band, and the shouter was none other than the bellicose guitarist, Louis.

Luke gritted his teeth. He cleared his throat.

"How are you, sir?" Luke said. He raised two fingers to his lowered forehead and flicked them at Louis. It was the world's most disrespectful salute.

"Bro, look at me when you speak to me!" Louis hurled up at them.

Luke's blue eyes pointed slowly at the guitarist.

"You're a fucking idiot mate," Louis shouted. "My amp shorted and it's worth three thousand dollars. It might never work again. Are you gonna pay for it?"

"No, why would I?" Luke answered.

Louis sprung off his little bench but the drummer, Hunter, grabbed him around the waist. The stupid mop-headed bass player sat with his arms crossed.

"Do I need to break this up again?" Bailey offered.

"No," Mark said. "Louis, calm down mate. I'll sort it out." Mark turned to Luke. "It wasn't actually *you* who threw the glass, was it?"

Luke was silent. Bailey was shaking her head.

"Who threw the glass?" Mark asked again.

"A glass was thrown," Nick said.

"Helpful," Luke muttered.

"We don't actually know," Bailey said, answering Mark's question. "We're not even sure if it was our friends. But it wasn't Luke."

"Why are you even sitting with them?" Louis shouted at Mark.

"I guess because he's alright," Mark said, but it was unclear to whom he referred.

"Aw, he's just trying to fuck that girl," Louis shouted, throwing up his arms and sitting.

Bailey blushed. But quietly she said, "Already done that." Bailey and Mark turned.

"*That girl* saved your life, you fucking bitch," Luke said to Louis, suddenly angry. "I'd show some gratitude if I were you."

Mark closed his eyes, praying his guitarist would bite his tongue. The truth was, Mark did not know why he was sitting at this table, and not at the other. He had come to this bougie bar with his band. But across drinkers he had seen Bailey, with her lengthy, dark hair, sitting with her blonde brother; and he had recognised Alan in their midst. Something had driven him to approach. Bailey had welcomed Mark to her table. He felt comfortable around her. And once Mark had sat, he had realised that, though he did not like Luke nor Nick, he liked Alan. Mark was unsure what it was. But a thought had come to him. Perhaps Alan reminded Mark of Jing Zhuang, Mark's dead father. There was something in the way Alan carried himself. He was quiet; he was humble. Mark's father had been just like that. And it wasn't as though Alan did not bear resemblance to Mark's father; although, as far as Mark knew, he had never seen photos of Jing Zhuang, and had very little to go by. Either way, it was true: Mark liked Alan. Did Alan like *Mark*? Mark had no idea.

Luke gulped obnoxiously at his Carlton Draught, and belched. He became subject to a sweep-over of Mark's narrowed eyes, an invasive sort of visual pat-down. "So, you didn't throw the glass. Okay." Mark exhaled smoke, and moralised: "Maybe you should choose your friends more wisely."

"Oh, c'mon bro. Get out of here. Who the fuck do you think you are? Do you think your friends are better than mine?" Luke made no effort to keep his voice down. "My friends aren't your friends, Mark. But they're cut from the same cloth. We all went to the same high schools, bruh. We're all giant douchebags."

Mark sipped at his Tallboy & Moose to stifle his anxiety. "Speak for yourself."

But Mark read Alan's silence as confirmation of Luke's accuracy.

"How's your hipster brew anyway?" Luke said.

"It's good mate," Mark answered. "You should try some."

Luke paused. Then he grabbed Mark's beer and slugged half of it down.

Luke coughed. "Tastes like shit."

"You like it," Bailey said. "You just drank half the glass."

Luke banged the glass down on the table. "Look, Mark, mate. Look. Now I know we've had a rocky start. But you know what mate?"

"What."

"We've been through the rocks."

"We've been round the twist," Mark said.

"We've been here and there, mate—"

"We've been up and down—"

"We've been all around. But you know what mate?"

"What."

"I'll tell you something," Luke said.

"What."

"I see you. I do, I see you. And you can do great things, my man."

"Oh for fuck's sake."

"You *can*. And you will. You'll do great things. You've got a fantastic ass—"

"His band's actually fucking good though," the red-head interjected.

"Thank you," Mark said.

"They're famous," Nick said, pointing across to where The Lights sat; though right now, the truth was that The Lights did not look very famous. Louis clenched his greasy hair in his fingers. Hunter thumbed his tiny iPhone with huge ferocity. The bass player, Keith, gawked across the bar at three Chinese women. There seemed to be a lot of empty space around The Lights.

"Well it took many years of hard yakka," Mark with his tiny moustache was saying. "And all our toils started to pay off. People finally started coming up to me when, like, I'd be out at a restaurant or something. But it was a long time coming. Like, we were writing songs in high school. And it wasn't until *last year* that all our elbow grease really started to pay off, you know? It wasn't really until we released—"

"If you're famous, I don't even know what I am," Luke spat.

"Well we're not talking about you, mate," Mark replied.

"Let him finish," Bailey told her brother.

"His head's so far up his ass his head's coming out of his head," Luke machine-gunned.

Mark froze. He gave a nervous and high-pitched laugh.

"He's laughing because he's recognising the truth in my words," Luke said.

"You're talking about yourself, though," Bailey said to Luke, and she put her hand on his finely-haired forearm.

"NO I'M NOT!" Luke bellowed, and everyone at the table jumped, and everyone in the bar heard him. Luke's blue eyes looked in the direction of his own forehead, and his mouth gaped like a cave.

"I don't know what to say," Mark murmured.

"*Famous, famous, famous!*" Luke screamed. "I sing about girls I've fucked in a fucking indie-rock band! We tour! Did I mention we tour!"

Mark smoked, watching Luke.

"*Please listen to my song!*" Luke went on, bringing his palms together and pretending to plead with a bewildered stranger at the next table. "I play in an indie-rock band. We're really good. I'll pay you to listen to my song! I'll *cry* if you *don't* listen to my song!" Luke would not stop; something had caught hold of his very soul.

The extent to which Luke had evidently read Mark had the latter floored. He was watching Luke, but the hard truth was that really, he was watching himself, as though in a mirror. And suddenly Mark understood everything. He shuddered. Not unlike many people Mark knew, Luke was a young man obsessed with the idea of fame. Luke was a comedian. Bailey had told Mark that the one thing Luke could not stand was low spirits in the people around him. And Mark could see that Luke believed his purpose was to make people laugh. But Luke had never performed. At what point, Mark wondered, had Luke decided on his occupation? Luke had decided; that much was clear. But Bailey had told Mark that Luke had never once stood upon a stage. According to Bailey, her brother had never so much as performed in a school play. Did this guy make videos? Did he perform stand-up routines privately for his friends? What made this broken boy with sandy hair and sky-blue eyes so sure of his profession? Mark could guess; Mark guessed it was the lights. The lights in his eyes, those eyes to the sky—and Mark watched Luke's sclerae tumefy. The lights were the dream; the dream was fame. Here was a boy who believed he had been born to do things the masses could not do. Here was a boy who would rather die than work a nine-to-five. Here was a boy who would murder a fellow human being in order to become famous.

Luke, still gesticulating like a machine with an overcharged battery, whacked his pint glass with his wild, beefy hand; the glass spun over the edge of the table like a gyroscope.

It was Alan who caught the glass before it hit the concrete.

"Time to go home," Alan smiled.

Alan placed the pint glass upright on the table and, abruptly, stood to leave.

"You're gonna leave just like that?" Luke said, shocked.

"Thank you for the beer," Alan smiled. "I enjoyed it very much."

Everyone shook Alan's hand and bid him goodbye.

"Hey, Alan," Mark said. "What's your number?"

Alan typed his phone number into Mark's caramel-leathered iPhone 7. He left the bar.

"I like that guy," Mark said, attempting to restart normal conversation.

"Yeah, I like him, too," Bailey said.

"You like everyone," Luke told her.

"Is that okay with you?" Bailey asked, looking at her brother.

"Oh, shit, he left his notebook," Mark said, and took his cigarette from his lips.

"No way!" Nick shouted.

"Er, I'm going to go and find him," Bailey said uneasily. "We should tell him—"

Bailey went through the glass door through which Alan had made his polite exit.

"Read it, read it," Luke said eagerly, but rain began to fall. "Read it to me. What does it say? Go to the first page and read it to me."

"Am I an audiobook?" Mark demanded, and carefully opened the tiny, grimy cover. Beneath it, the first page was loose, and it nearly fell out. It was raining properly now, and every other punter was departing the outdoor area of the bar. Nick shouted to them from indoors.

But Luke sprang up and crouched by Mark in the downpour. The two of them cupped their hands around the notebook, attempting in earnest to protect it from water-damage.

They squinted in silence.

Finally Mark swore.

"Holy. Fucking. Shit."

"That's *amazing*. I really like that."

"Dude. Holy shit."

"It's good isn't it?"

"That's probably the best thing I've ever read."

"That *is* the best thing I've ever read."

"And so—different."

"So perfect."

"Oh my God, man."

"Who *is* this guy?"

Chapter 4

And then the virus hit. COVID-19 was not very good for the depressed. It is said that the pandemic of 2019-2021 caused more deaths via suicide than via the coronavirus. On the 11th of March 2020, what had been news of a mysterious bat in Wuhan escalated to the World Health Organisation's declaration of global disaster. Like everywhere else, Melbourne began to close its schools and to order work from home; many of the infected perished; in all truth, nobody had any idea what was happening. 20,000 Melburnians caught the virus and 800 of them died from complications. Thousands and thousands of others went out of their minds.

That was what happened to the writer, to the musician, and to the comedian.

Alan's job prospects disappeared and his plans to take a bed in a west-side apartment were destroyed. People looked at him differently. Alan could defend himself. But he did not like to be told to return to China. Alan had never been to China. He kept his eyes on the pavement when he walked and on his notebooks when he sat. And he filled those notebooks faster than he had filled them in all his twenty-five long years. He knew he had filled hundreds in his lifetime. The streets owned most of them; Alan never carried more than a handful. The writings he deemed worthy were transcribed and uploaded by him to a secret and untraceable Tumblr page; the page had procured a small and gently-growing following. Alan never responded to comments. But he checked the page as though it were cigarettes. As for the writings that did not make the cut, they filled notebooks left by Alan on shining café tables, in the trunks of sighing trees, in the centre of dark and momentarily vacant highways past midnight. They were read. It was only when Alan was sure his writings could not be traced back to their author that he allowed this. As such, it had not been his intention to misplace his notebook under the pointed privileged noses of Mark and Luke. Bailey had caught him in a twinkling rain-drenched street, and in him her words had ignited something huge and precarious. They had returned to the bar to find the notebook essentially unreadable; Mark and Luke fervently promised Alan both that they had done all that was in their power to protect it from the deluge, which, as Luke insisted, fell at the wildest of angles, and, moreover, that of course they had not dreamed of opening its cover; the case being, on the contrary, that from the moment Mark and Luke had laid eyes on Alan's black scrawl, each was convinced of the same thing: Alan was of a separate realm. This silent writer, with his scarred lips and affable expression, was going to *make it*. Neither Mark nor Luke were interested in poetry. In all truth, Luke despised poetry. And yet, it could not have been clearer, to Luke, nor to Mark; and nobody was more sensitive to the seeds of true and unstoppable talent than they were. Alan was going to become famous.

'Intimate partners' was one of the small number of categories created and permitted by the Australian government to visit during the long months of enforced social distancing. The ruling drew Mark and Bailey closer. The pandemic nourished their love. Yet the singer in the band began to withdraw. An East Coast tour, what would have been the band's third, was cancelled.

Government funding for The Arts was cut significantly. The Lights did not meet. The only interactions Mark had were with his lifeless housemates and with Bailey. But he required more. Mark was filled with wandering, tempestuous rage at the agonising irony that, unlike in the case of the bushfires earlier that year (not to suggest, however, that he had particularly cared about those relief efforts), the absolute most effective thing he could do to help accelerate the end of the crisis was to lock himself in his bedroom and do the absolute least amount of stuff. But even the torture of social isolation was not the foremost reason for Mark's withdrawal. The foremost reason for Mark's withdrawal was his newfound conviction, in the wake of that day at that Southbank bar, that he was untalented. He would never play music the way Alan wrote poetry. It was as simple as that. Even Luke's stupid Trump take had been too much for Mark to handle.

And the pandemic hit no one harder than it hit Lucas Weir. The comedian obstinately refused to follow a single one of the brand-new laws. No one was quite sure why. Luke visited his friends. Luke hugged and kissed. Luke would never don a mask. It was as though the boy was in denial of the virus' existence. He told his parents COVID-19 was a "*problem for the privileged*". Of the members of their household, it was only Bailey who tolerated Luke's insanity. Yet Luke hated his younger sister for loving the spineless singer of The Lights; when the topic arose, it was the look in Bailey's eyes that sent Luke over the edge. "*I love you too*," Bailey urged her brother. "*I hate you*," Luke replied. Luke stopped talking to Bailey altogether. The day Luke went missing, Bailey drove to Mark's house and cried into his tattooed arms.

*

It was night time in Elizabeth Street. Nearly invisible, Alan sped down the tiled pavement, his hands in his pockets. Bad music pounded ahead. Alan raised his black-hooded head to see someone fall into a side-street out of an explosion of light. The man was white, with shoulder-length and greasy black hair, and his face was knotted into a frantic expression of joy. Alan began to cross Elizabeth Street, but the greasy-haired man was shouting at him. The shouting was hoarse the way the voice of someone who has been shouting for several hours is hoarse. The door out of which the man had fallen slammed shut.

"Fuck it's good to see someone out and about. I've had a big night, nah, no parties, nothing like that, I was just in there with myself and no one else. Like, I was just having a one-man solo party in my lonesome, and I kicked myself out of it for going a bit hard, like, sometimes you gotta get heavy-handed, gotta do what you gotta do, like, someone's going a bit hard, someone's just sending it, you gotta do what you gotta do, so I kicked myself out of my own party. I know, it sounds like there are people in there, and the music sounds pretty loud, doesn't it? But nah I was just... Okay you got me, there's a party in there, and I was at it, but don't look at me like I'm the only one going to parties alright? I know you wouldn't judge me. Sorry, I'm gacked off my tits, mate, I hope you don't mind... you seem like a really nice guy. That's so important these days, it's like everyone's forgotten how to be nice. Like, every day, it's like temperature's rising, you know what I mean?, like Trump gets in a little bit of riff-raff with Kim Jong-un, next thing you know Kim Jong-un's launching nuclear missiles at America, China's getting in on it, meanwhile ScoMo's off on holiday in Hawaii or something doing sweet fuck-all. It's hard times, people are saying the coronavirus changed the world, but really the coronavirus only dug all the problems up that were already there just lying under the surface, like, it's not long until World War Three, and I know I'm not the only one who sees it coming, this virus is only the beginning of all the crazy shit that's gonna befall us in the coming years, man. So you make the most of the moment while you're young. But I really appreciate how much of a nice guy you are, like I just got kicked out, like kicked myself out of my own party, and it's like people have forgotten how to just relax a little bit and have a little bit of fun, you know?, everyone's so serious with all this lockdown bullshit, but *I* haven't got the virus, no one's actually *got* the virus, and I was only talking to that chick, I wouldn't have done anything to her, I was just having a laugh and they get all fucking serious. The world needs more people like you. What's your name? Alan, you fucking legend, it's nice to meet you man. Jayden's what they call me. You probably already knew that, my reputation's probably preceded me, I'm well-known in this city, I'm friends with a lot of powerful people, haha, The Smith Street Band, you know them? I'm good friends with Wil, we go way back. By the way, are you homeless? There are so many fucking hobos in this area man, I'm not judging, I'm not judging, but look at that guy in that alley, like, at least keep yourself clean-shaven, or just lose a little weight or something, like, there comes a time to take the reins of your own life, and like, somehow this guy's missed the boat. And look at this guy, he's just destroying his own life, you know what I mean?, and that red hat's probably the only fucking thing he owns, and he probably stole it too, haha! Like I'm not judging—"

"I found you!" somebody screamed, and Jayden squealed in terror, and Alan leapt back. Alan peered deeper into the alley to see two white orbs emerge from the darkness. These were a man's eyes pointed directly skyward, so that whatever irises the man possessed were completely obscured by the broad forehead, leaving only the bottom half of the milky and capillary-cracked sclerae visible between the eyelids. Now Alan saw this man was dressed entirely in black: bulky black boots, billowing black cloth trousers, and a giant black nylon puffer jacket covered in holes and rips. The colossal sleeves of the puffer jacket were pushed back to the elbows, and dark, ominous lacerations lined the forearms. Both of the man's big hands were waving at Alan, as though the man were some psychotic clown, and the frenzied face was hidden behind a jungle of twisted and blonde-coloured hair.

"You've been in my visions Alan!" the man screamed, and Alan gaped. "The visions told me I was gonna find you here, and the visions never lie! I've been looking all over for you in these streets, I owe everything to you, here, listen to me, we've got so much to talk about. The world is falling apart! You saved my life, and I've been out here for several seasons looking for you mate, having visions about you, nah like don't think I'm stalking you or anything but I've been playing it cool, just having visions about you and tracking you down so I can find you because I need to repay you for what you did for me. You saved my life, it's because of you that I'm here! What can I *do* for you? Let me give you something! Here, you can have all the money I've got in my wallet, I'm serious. Please. I've got... Alan, when the bars open up again I'm gonna do an open-mic night, I'm gonna do it, I don't care if getting up there makes me a pretentious asshole, I *am* a pretentious asshole, I know it but I don't care, I'll force my jokes down their throats so that either they're gonna laugh or they're gonna suffocate! I'm gonna be the best fucking stand-up comedian the country's ever seen. And you're gonna be huge, you're gonna be the most famous writer since like, Murakami—I ran away from home, I abandoned everyone for my career, I abandoned everyone for Lucas Weir, I cut my sister off, she calls me every day, but I don't wanna hear it, so I leave her on '*read*'. Every day she's just crying. But I don't wanna hear it man! It's just me and these streets now, because I was born into the worst possible circumstances a person can be born into, I was born into *privilege*, and I don't deserve any of that, I cut myself off from all of that to *teach myself*. These deserted streets are hacking off my privilege man, they're keeping me down and depressed, because it's my duty to keep myself as depressed as I possibly can, Alan, like, depression is the pathway to stardom, and it's either I'm gonna be a famous comic or I'm gonna fucking kill myself, that's it, that's all there is. I've already tried eight times, they came to my house and they took me away and they locked me up, and I got out and it was then that I realised my career's all I've got left mate, this path I'm walking down is the only path left for me, as all around this path the world falls apart. They're saying there's a virus that's gonna infect us and kill us, well I know you're too smart to go along with that mainstream account, I've *seen* you in my *visions* mate and I know you've got your head screwed on right, you know they're playing us so they can control us, because that's all Dandrews wants, to keep us under his boot, to control us, control!, that's all he wants and I know you know this already and don't need me to tell you. Who's your friend?"

"Well you're fucking crazy mate," Jayden began. "But I can get down with one thing you said. This virus might just be a hoax."

"What's your name man?"

"Jay."

"Jay, it *is* a hoax. I can promise you that the coronavirus is about as real as the fucking boogeyman—"

"I'm so glad you think so because—"

"Oh, I know so, Jay."

"Like I'm so glad you know so because sometimes it's like no one will listen to me!" Jayden shouted. "I've been saying this shit this whole time, the virus can't be real because why would we just take their word for it, and just change the way we live our lives and stop going out and doing what we have a right to do just because someone we haven't even met told us there's a coronavirus that will kill us if we catch it? Sorry, sorry, fellas, I've had a big night, I had too many caps and I'm chewing your bloody ears off but at least some people are nice, like, you know what I mean?, Alan's so nice, you can tell as soon as you meet him, and that's so important these days. Anyway, I'm sure my reputation preceded me. I'm in with some very important people, like you know the Smith Street Band?, yeah of course you do, well I'm in with Wil, I've known him since 2010, like we go way back, and I'm *known* in this city, like, you know The Lights? You know the alt-rock band The Lights? They did that song, *Eyes to the Sky*, you know, '*Those eyes to the skyyy*', yeah!, yeah of course you know that song. Yeah we go way back, but like, you know they're not even legit right? Like, this is just what I heard, and nah like don't think I'm not gonna have my mates' backs, like *nah* like don't think for a *second* I'm not here for them, 'cos I am, we go *waaay* back, but I'm just saying, like, and this is just what I heard, but I'm just saying, some of The Lights are fucking scumbags, man. Oh, something about their success, and how it's not actually legit. What do I mean? Oh, just that I've heard some very fucking sketchy things about The Lights, man, and these are all just rumours anyway. Like, these are my boys, so I've probably dug myself into a bit of a hole. Well, I'm not one to spread rumours, maybe I should stop. And these are my fellas, me and them go way back, like Hunter's my boy through and through, Mark too, but you know Louis? And this is just what I've heard, so I'm probably wrong, and I fucking *hope* I'm wrong. And don't fucking tell anyone any of what I'm about to say, okay? This is between the three of us, because I like the both of you and because the both of you seem nice and because I'm in a good mood. This doesn't leave this street corner, okay? You didn't hear this from me. All I heard was that the guitarist of The Lights, Louis, okay, all I heard was that he's a complete fucking parasite of a human being, like he's responsible for the success of *Eyes to the Sky* because what he did was—I don't know if this is true, so just—but what I heard was that what Louis did, right, was he—basically he lives with his mum and doesn't have a job, right, sits at his mum's house for ten hours a day just making fake Instagram accounts, making fake Facebook accounts, making fake YouTube accounts, he sits there with no shirt—I don't know if the no-shirt part is true—but he sits there and makes thousands and thousands of these fake accounts and he goes on the pages of other bands and other artists and he '*dislikes*' their videos on YouTube, he hits like that '*thumbs-down*' button with all of these fake accounts, he writes hate-mail on various online platforms, like for real, he goes on the Facebook pages of other artists in the scene and does like that '*haha*' reaction, you know like with the '*haha*' emoji, all of this shit so that other bands look bad on social media. And he uses these fake accounts and he '*likes*' all of The Lights' posts and photos and shit, and he goes on Spotify and plays his own songs over and over again with his finger, tapping and tapping so the play-count of The Lights' songs gets to like a million, whatever. Like, I understand a fledgling artist paying one of those Indian companies to rack them up fake likes and fake plays, like it's a cut-throat fucking industry these days and you gotta spend money to get money, you know?, you gotta do what you gotta do, but what Louis does is like a whole 'nother level. And like, writing fake hate mail to Rolling Blackouts Coastal Fever, you know Rolling Blackouts Coastal Fever?, like writing Rolling Blackouts Coastal Fever hate-mail from hundreds of separate non-existent fucking social media accounts, like you have to be a very special type of fucking parasite cunt to do that, and I don't know, like I said, I'll always have Hunter's back—"

"Had a bit to drink tonight, boys, have we?"

Jayden had been cut off mid-sentence by the deep voice of a blue-clad policeman, who had rounded the corner of Lonsdale Street.

"Nah mate, of course not, what do you—"

"You shouldn't be outside of your home," a second, stockier policeman said.

"We don't have any home to go to, sir," Luke said to the second policeman, gripping Alan by the shoulder. "We were just going for a bit of a stroll. We don't know this guy."

Jayden froze and stared googly-eyed at Luke.

"But dude, we go way back!" Jayden protested. Even in the darkness, it was easy to see Jayden's pupils were the size of golf cups.

"We're gonna need to breathalyse you, mate," the stockier policeman said quietly.

Jayden sprinted off into the night, his greasy hair flicking backward. The policemen ran up Lonsdale Street towards their car. Luke and Alan stood in silence. They watched the police car howl around the empty corner and shoot down Elizabeth Street after the doomed drug-user.

"Would you fancy that," Luke said.

"Ha," Alan said.

They stood on the black street corner. Their dim shadows loomed under the streetlights. The pedestrian-crossing buttons produced hollow clinking noises.

"I always knew there was something wrong with The Lights," Luke said, slowly at first. "But this is... well, I mean, it makes total sense. I will say this, man, that's a weird friend you've got there."

"I don't know him."

"But you know, Alan, I've been out here for several seasons, roaming these streets. And I've been looking for you. Because I'm just such a... terrible, terrible person, and you're such a good genuine person. And I've finally realised it's my duty to give thanks to the people who I need to give thanks to. Please, Alan. Take all the money I've got." Alan looked down; Luke was holding his hefty wallet in his right hand, and several banknotes in his left. Luke shoved the wallet back into his baggy black trousers and began to count the money. "I've got... six hundred and twenty dollars on me. It's yours mate. Take it." Luke grabbed Alan's hand and placed the cash into it.

"No, please, it's your money," Alan said, mortified.

"*It's your money.*" Luke closed Alan's hand around the slippery cash and physically forced the hand into the torn pocket of Alan's hoodie. Alan did not have a say.

"I don't want it."

"Take it anyway. What else can I do for you, brother? Anything you like, you name it. You saved my life."

"Please, I don't want anything."

"Just let me do something for you. But how about The fucking Lights though, huh?" Luke's dingo laugh exploded from his throat. "Can you fucking believe it, man? What a bunch of..." Luke stopped, as though he were deep in thought. "It's all true though. Of course everything your weird friend said about The Lights is true. You can tell it's all true right?"

"Who knows if it is true."

"Alan, you're too nice, can't you see it's the reason they've made it so big all over the Internet? It's all fake. Those motherfuckers will never know what it truly is to truly be successful. *You* will. You're gonna be *huge*, you're gonna be a famous author. I know this 'cos I've *seen* you, man, I had a vision the other day and the whole room was gold, like gold-plated walls, gold-plated bookshelves, this gold-and-crystal chandelier, and *there you were*, sitting at this *epic* like mahogany writing desk, and you were wearing like a diamond necklace and you were writing ground-breaking poetry with a quill made from the feather of an endangered parrot. And to your left was this *hectic* like diamond-studded fireplace, and there was like this *screaming*, man, and I looked into the fireplace and I was burning to death in the fire. Haha! But nah, I'm gonna be the most famous goddamn comedian in the whole goddamn world. Or else I'm gonna die... But The Lights, man, The Lights are the shining example of what happens when you just get *too obsessed* chasing fame. That cunt is the absolute worst kind of sick motherfucker. I'm talking about that fuckwit guitarist. He owes his life to my sister! And don't think for a second I don't love my sister, man. I told you I cut her off, and I leave her on '*read*', but don't think for even a second I don't love my sister. Fucking Louis will never understand what it is to *pay back your debts*. We would have beaten that piece of shit to death if Bailey hadn't walked up on that stage and told us to back off. We would've killed him, and I wish we had, the world would have been a better place if Bailey hadn't been so fucking blindly compassionate. We would've killed that piece of shit. And Louis knows he owes Bailey his life, but rather than thanking her for his *life*, man, he's sitting at home literally concocting synthetic fame for himself. Dude, fuck The Lights. Are you with me? Dude. Alan. Do you want me to kill them?" Suddenly Luke began to laugh like a maniac. "I'll kill them. You want me to?"

"No," Alan replied, and stopped walking. "I have to go now."

"*Don't go!*" Luke screamed, seizing Alan by the arm yet again. "Just let me settle my debts, man! What do you want? I'll do anything for you my brother, I owe you my life. Do you want me to kill Mark?"

"Luke." Alan forced himself to look up into Luke's shining eyes. "You want to do something for me, right?"

"Yes. Anything."

"You want to thank me."

"I want to give you my deepest and most eternal thanks. I owe you—"

"Don't kill Mark. Don't kill anyone. Calm down."

Alan held on to Luke's fevered gaze.

"You want me to—"

"I want you... to not kill anyone. Okay?"

Luke stared into Alan's dark eyes.

Chapter 5

But COVID-19 just kept spreading, dragging Luke through the dirt behind it. The comedian and five of his friends found Mark on his twilight walk in Edinburgh Gardens. Mark froze when he saw them.

"Where's Louis?" Luke shouted.

"Fellas—"

"Don't '*fellas*' me. Where's Louis?"

"Why do you want Louis?"

"I've got personal business with him. And I know the truth about your band, Mark. I know what Louis does."

"What are you talking about?"

"I know how you made it so big! I know about your *tactics*."

"Luke, Jesus, what's happened to you?"

Suddenly Max had the singer in a headlock. Luke ignored Mark's surprise and punched Mark's pencil moustache as hard as he could. Mark screamed. The rest of Luke's huge friends had assembled around them in a circle.

"*Where does Louis live?*" Luke demanded.

Mark blubbered in pain. "Luke, whatever problem you have with Louis, you can sort it out, like, is this about Bail—"

Luke swung his fist up into Mark's stomach. Mark buckled slightly against Max's restraint. Luke stepped toward Mark until Mark felt Luke's breath hot on his bleeding mouth. Mark scrunched his eyes shut in disgust.

"What's wrong, Mark?" Luke leered. "Am I too close for your comfort? Would you like me to respect *social distancing*?"

Several of Luke's friends snickered. Mark had no idea what to do.

"Open your eyes, bitch," Luke said.

Slowly, Mark forced his eyes open. He barely recognised this monster. Luke's blue irises shimmered out of an onslaught of overgrown blonde facial hair.

"You're untalented," Luke said, his breath pounding into Mark's face. "Your band is untalented. You don't deserve the recognition you've gotten, and you know it." And as Luke said these words, Mark watched the sky-blue irises rise, and keep rising, until the irises were far too high, up behind the blonde eyebrows, and Luke's eyes were entirely white.

"Okay, you're right!" Mark cried. "We suck!"

Luke's blue irises descended. Luke stared down at the singer.

"You suck," Luke breathed.

"We suck!"

Luke grinned.

"So why don't you tell me where Louis lives?"

"I can't just tell you where Louis *lives*!"

Luke grinned into Mark's eyes. Then he stepped backward. He broke eye contact with Mark to make eye contact with Max.

"Let him go," Luke said.

Max released his captive. Mark held at his bruised stomach.

"One on one," Luke said quietly. "I won't let my boys hit you. I wanna have you to myself. Hit me."

Mark looked up at Luke.

"No."

"I said *hit me* bitch!"

"I don't wanna fight man!"

"For fuck's sake. Look around you. There are six of us. If you don't hit me, Mark, *we'll all hit you.*"

Mark did not have a choice. He removed his glittering ring from his pinkie finger and placed it in his left pocket; one of Luke's bodyguards sniggered again. Mark took a deep breath, and swung his right hand at Luke's cheek. But to his disbelief, Luke did not defend himself from the attack. Mark's fist went right into Luke's cheek and the hairy head flipped to the left. Mark stared.

"Hit me again."

"Dude, hit him back," Luke's even-blonder friend urged Luke.

"*C'mon man,*" another friend pled.

But suddenly Luke stared once again at Mark. "I said *hit me again!*"

Mark squeezed his throbbing fist and hurled it at Luke's cheek again. This was a much more controlled blow. Accompanying the thud was a horrifying crack.

"Hahahaha!" Luke screamed, clearly on another planet. And then Luke was bashing at Mark with his giant fists, bashing and bashing, and Mark was utterly helpless, trying in vain to shield himself, crouched down on the damp grass. Luke sat on top of Mark and hit him across the ears, in his jaw, in his left eye. Luke used his right elbow to bludgeon Mark's chest. Luke jumped off Mark, stood over him, and kicked him several times with his rocky black boots: in Mark's stomach, in Mark's crossed forearms, in Mark's head. Then Luke bent toward the sobbing singer.

"Know this, Mark," Luke spat. "It's really important that you know this. You owe your life to someone now. Do you know why?

Nah, you don't know why, but you're going to know why, because I'm about to tell you. And it's really important that you understand this. You owe your life to Alan Zhang. Because if Alan Zhang hadn't asked me to spare you..." (Luke gestured to his hulking bodyguards) "...we would've fucking killed you. Remember that, Mark. You owe your life to someone now."

Mark was in hospital when his test came back positive; four out of Luke's five friends tested positive; the blondest of Luke's friends, Sam, tested negative; Luke did not get tested. Luke's fever took hold hours after leaving Edinburgh Gardens. He rode it out in his goose-down Eddie Bauer Airbender sleeping bag, spread out in a hard ditch near the heaving Yarra. He curled up and coughed and immersed himself in his visions, in which he saw himself, suffering from a surprisingly bad cold, engulfed in flames in his thousand-dollar sleeping bag. He watched himself moan and shudder, he watched the white skin of his face melt in the flames, he watched himself scream away the final minutes of his life, he watched himself die, he watched the flames lower, and then he watched his blue eyes reopen and the flames reignite and the face-melting resume and the screaming restart and he watched this cycle over and over like a YouTube video on eternal repeat.

Mark was initially diagnosed, among other things, with tracheobronchial injury, three broken ribs, a shattered nose, a fractured left ulna, and concussion. He was tested procedurally for COVID-19 upon admittance to the Intensive Care Unit of St. Vincent's Department of Critical Care Medicine; as expected the test came back negative. But on his third day in the bed, his respiratory condition began to worsen. He was administered a second test, and his doctors and nurses alike were horrified when the lab declared their patient positive. Mark was immediately transferred to the hospital's isolated COVID-19 specialist centre; he was coughing blood. The coronavirus compounded the rupture of Mark's right main bronchus, resulting in severe respiratory failure and hypoxaemia. He was fully sedated and placed under extracorporeal membrane oxygenation. Mark was dying.

In seething moments of tormented semiconsciousness, Mark learned he had contracted the virus, and knew beyond all doubt who was to blame.

Chapter 6

"Baby."

"Bailey."

"Oh my God, baby, you're alive."

"I'm alive."

"Oh my God, Mark, I knew you were going to make it! I've tried to see you every day."

"I know, they told me."

"It's so good to hear your voice."

"I feel the same way, Bailey. Have you been sick?"

"I haven't. We were together right after you were exposed—"

"When you drove me to the hospital. You kept kissing me."

"I know, but it doesn't get contagious that quickly."

"Are you sure? You don't feel anything?"

"I don't feel anything. Just love for you. I'm so happy you're in recovery baby. Your nurses update me every day, they tell me everything, and you're gonna be okay."

"...I might never sing again."

"...I didn't hear that. Did they tell you that?"

"I can feel it."

"Have you asked your doctors?"

"They said it should be fine, but I can just feel it."

"It'll be okay, Mark. And he definitely didn't intend that."

"You know it's normal to attribute blame sometimes, right?"

"He didn't know—"

"*He gave me fucking COVID*, Bailey. I don't care if he knew he had it or not."

"You have every right to blame him for what he did. But he didn't intend to *kill* you. He had no idea he had the virus, he had no idea he was giving it to you. You know that's what happened right? That's why you nearly..."

"Yeah, my right main bronchus."

"But you're gonna be okay. Mark, Luke didn't want to *kill* you."

"I think he *did* though, Bailey. I've never seen someone like that. Have you seen him?"

"No! I haven't seen him since he ran away. He doesn't—he doesn't—he doesn't wanna talk to me."

"When I saw him, he was like another person, like, unshowered, filthy, and just *non compos mentis*, like, I still don't know why he wanted to kill me, but he did, I think he had some problem with *Louis* or something, I'm gonna call him later... and he mentioned that writer guy too, Alan... he wanted me to tell him where Louis lives, like, I'm serious, he was trying to get Louis's address out of me! And I guess he was angry about us. Are you crying?"

"*Yes*, I'm crying."

"...I love you, Bailey."

"I love you too, Mark."

"I love you, Bailey. But I'm not just gonna let this go. Luke nearly took my life away from me. What he said to me was, '*If Alan Zhang hadn't asked me to spare you, we would've killed you.*' That was what he said to me."

"Alan Zhang?"

"Alan Zhang, that writer guy. Like, are they even friends? It's so confusing. But I've gotta talk to Louis, and I've gotta talk to Alan, and I've gotta—I've gotta—"

"Baby, how could you *possibly* get Luke back for this?"

"Well, I don't know Bailey, I could kill him!"

"...Okay, do that."

"I could kill him."

"Mark, you're not gonna kill him. First of all, no one knows where he is. Second of all, if you actually did manage to find him, and you tried something, what do you seriously think would happen?"

"I'll kill him."

"MARK! Fuck, Mark. Be better than him. Okay? He'd kill you!"

"I don't care."

"See? You're not thinking straight. You just expressed to me that you *do* care, alright, you value your life, you're happy you're alive."

"I don't care..."

"You're gonna be okay, but you're not gonna be okay if you try to get Luke back for this."

"...Hhh."

"So call Louis and call Alan. And forgive Luke."

"Forgive him."

"Forgive him."

"Forgive him?"

"That's what I said. He doesn't know what he's doing. He's lost himself, like, he's a *victim*."

"Bailey, are you actually—"

"Remember why you're here. And I don't mean in the hospital. I mean on Earth."

"*Huh?*"

"You're here because of love. Remember when you told me that? You're here because of love, you're alive because of universal love. That's what you told me. That's why you do what you do. That's why you play your music. That's why you write all your wonderful songs. That's why you sing."

"Okay, what the fuck does that have to do with it?"

"Right? You're alive because of love."

"I want love."

"You want universal love. I think this is your moment, Mark. Have you thought about *giving* love?"

"Bailey—"

"I'm serious."

"He nearly killed me."

"That's what I'm saying."

Mark rose into consciousness, claustrophobic in his unforgiving bed, nearly immobilised by a treacherous infrastructure of invasive medical intervention, and fell into oblivion. Awake, Mark stewed; asleep, Mark seethed. The virus began to leave his fragile body. His breathing began to improve. But Mark was held fast. Unless he was speaking on the phone, or else responding to the directions and questions of his caregivers, Mark was silent. He was not himself. Silence was not in his blood. He scrolled through his iPhone. He listened to every piece of music recorded in the twentieth and twenty-first centuries, yet denied himself permission to hum along with a single tune. Despite his doctor's promise, Mark knew he would never sing again. Physically, he was regaining health. Psychologically, he was not.

Until the day Marcus Tze received what would be his final positive test result. He did not know how long he had been in the hospital; he did not know how long he had had COVID-19; he did not know that beyond the windowless white walls of the specialist centre within which he lived what would for evermore be the largest day of his life, the winter sun blazed. He simply gave up. He would never understand Bailey, he would never understand the reassurance in her voice. He opened his hand.

Mark had never witnessed talent as real as Alan's. Over whatever the period of time was that he had so far been incapacitated, Mark had tried more than ten times to call Alan's phone number. He had sent Alan several text messages. There had been no response. Bailey had, however, managed to find Alan camouflaged away in one of the slowly-repopulating streets of Melbourne's central business district (from what Mark had heard, state-wide case numbers had now lowered sufficient for the squint-eyed Premier of Victoria to permit cautious loosening of his lockdown regulations). Bailey had learned from Alan that what Luke had told Mark had been true. Alan was responsible for Mark's life. Mark had tried by every means to express his gratitude to Alan. But for all he knew, Alan did not have mobile phone access. So Mark went ahead. In what seemed like another age, that raining February day before the pandemic, at that ritzy bar in Southbank, Mark and Luke had read Alan's black poetry within the wetted pages of his crumbling notebook. Like Luke, Mark had been struck breathless by what he saw. Mark had been so deeply moved by the poetry that, against his better conscience, he had photographed three of the writings, seconds before they had been rendered illegible by the lashing rain. And now, upright in his white hospital bed, Mark transcribed the infallible and golden poetry into his iPhone's Notes app. He spent several minutes with his eyes closed, his tattooed forefinger poised, simply breathing. And then he opened Instagram. He found the official Instagram page of the Canadian poet, Rupi Kaur, whom he had met on a handful of occasions and who had expressed enthusiasm for The Lights' EP. And he typed up a well-worded Direct Message. Essentially, my friend is more talented than I will ever be. His name is Alan Zhang, and here is his work. It would mean so much to me if you would take the time to read it.

But no!, Mark swiped his Instagram window up and away. He could not press the tiny blue paper plane symbol. Alan's consent was first required. But how to obtain it? Mark would—somehow. And as soon as the author's consent had been granted, the infinite gift would be given; and if, by some impiety, Kaur failed to see the obvious, Mark would send Alan's poetry to others. Mark knew several writers and publishers; and it barely mattered to whom, specifically, he sent these literary fireworks now on the countdown within the caramel-leathered iPhone in his shaking hand. Destiny knew no obstacle. Alan would be a star.

But that part would be the deepest of pleasures. And this part would be pain.

Mark opened his Photos app. He scrolled down to Recently Deleted. Here were rows and rows of bad photographs of debauched nights and otherwise-repressed memories. For months, just the way a sorry gambler plaps at his spectral slot machine, Mark had neurotically Recovered and re-Deleted and re-Recovered the 28-second video. He played it for the last time. *"...'I do cherish women! I love women!' My mother was like the greatest woman I've ever met!..."* For the last time, Mark experienced that gut-wrenching horror he had experienced when he had watched the clip take place. Luke was not an artist. But his Donald Trump impression was on-point. Mark felt sick. He did not understand why he was doing what he was doing.

Chapter 7

There was something about Bailey that made Alan happy. Alan was unused to happiness. He had been under the cover of a tiny carpark in the right angle of some alley, and she had power-walked toward him, and Alan had seen her hips-length hair move. Just before Alan had turned away, Bailey had smiled. And facing the wall, Alan had smiled too. Alan had cautiously answered Bailey's impassioned questions about her brother, had received without reaction Bailey's account of Luke's assault on Mark, and had confirmed that, when Luke had insisted upon paying him some favour, he had asked Luke to have mercy on the musician. According to Bailey, her beloved Mark had been trying to get in contact with Alan; Alan said that he accepted Mark's gratitude, that Bailey was welcome to pass this on to Mark, that his mobile phone had long ago been swapped for Champion Ruby, and that when Alan had replaced the phone, he had not bothered to pay for a new plan. Bailey had then asked to add Alan on Facebook, and Alan had agreed, conceding Facebook Messenger to be the most reliable (or, Bailey guessed, the *least unreliable*) way to contact him in future. Bailey had given Alan a sleek black ballpoint pen, engraved on the plunger's tip with a tiny red love heart. She had swivelled her agile lips to invite from Alan an affectionate kiss on the cheek, and stood to leave the alley.

So it was that when, through Facebook Messenger, Alan received a message from Bailey, the writer's hollow soul seemed to fill with light. It was love, but it was not like the love Alan had once known in now long-dead relationships. It was something like friendship. Alan loved Bailey as though she were a friend; and a buried part of him hoped that that was what she would become. Another part of Alan hoped that his surmise as to the reason for Bailey's contact would prove wrong. Leaning against the Sandridge Bridge parapet, Alan read the message.

> *Hey Alan! :) How are you? Listen, you know how I was saying Mark wanted to thank you for what you did for him? Well he wants me to ask you whether he can maybe help you with your career. He's read your poetry and wants to send it to his friend who's an influential poet, Rupi Kaur was who he had in mind. Have you read her work? We feel like she's the perfect person, all she needs to do is share 2 or 3 of your amazing poems on her Instagram page, and the rest will be history. You'll go viral! Obviously it's your choice and he wouldn't want to do this if you weren't completely comfortable with it. How would you feel about it? Let me know, love <3 Bailey*

But at "*influential poet*", Alan had shut his eyes and dropped his Telstra Essential into the brown Yarra. Alan instantly knew that Mark had already sent his poetry to whoever Mark's icon friend was; how Mark had obtained copies of Alan's poetry was a question Alan did not want answered. Bailey, with her keen emotional intelligence and her infinite goodness, was asking permission too late. This was not conjecture. Alan knew intuitively that the deed had been done.

(It had not.)

Alan stared into the pulsing Yarra. Love; it was all love. He removed the contents of the torn front pocket of his black hoodie: a flimsy notebook, and the pen with the love heart. He opened the notebook and filled three of its pages. He closed the notebook and closed his eyes. And then, at last, he stepped down the bridge towards the city. He walked slowly. For the first time in months, he walked with his head held high, though he did not make eye contact with any of the people who passed him by. Neither did he hear the traffic surrounding him. He heard Bailey's sincere voice; it calmed him. But the nausea came on. On the final street, he quickened. He looked up and the sunlight caught his dark eye, and beyond it, he saw his destination. It was so beautiful, it was all love! There was no time to lose. Alan entered the abandoned skyscraper. He stepped over the neglected steel concreting mesh toward the staircase. Oh, how he loved this stone staircase. He climbed and climbed, stepping over the rotting timber planks, ducking under the fallen pillars. And then he was on the flat roof. He walked to the edge, where he had stood so many times. He gazed down at his beloved streets and did not vomit. With both hands, he squeezed the notebook and the pen together in his pocket. Alan raised his eyes to the blinding sky and stepped off the stone edge of the roof. The rushing air burned at his eyes, but he focussed all of his energy upon trying in vain to hold them open and upon squeezing the notebook together with Bailey's pen. The poetry would be read and Alan would be dead. Alan smiled and smashed into the pavement.

But Alan's poetry would never really be read. Mark never sent Alan's poems to Rupi Kaur. And the notebook and the pen in Alan's pocket were confiscated, and ultimately, disposed of.

Bunkered under a granite-tiled platform in the foetal position, Luke had watched the distant thing step off the decrepit stone tower in his vision's right and fall directly left so that it disappeared behind another building. Luke had pitied it. Now he wriggled out into the light, leaving his foul-smelling belongings behind him in his lair. Hands in his pockets, he moseyed the blocks between himself and his vague notion of the landing-place. He found a small circle of distraught pedestrians on Queen Street, who cleared out of Luke's way like repulsed magnets.

The body was wrecked but suddenly Luke recognised Alan's scarred face. Luke's iPhone 11 Pro Max rang in his pocket and he fell to his knees.

"Alan! Oh, no fucking way. Alan, what are you doing? *Alan*! Why'd you do that? Alan, why'd you do that? No way, I just, sorry, I know him, I just can't... Alan! Oh for fuck's sake, what the fuck mate, Alan, you can't be serious mate, why would you do that. *Alan*!"

But Luke did not hear his phone ringing, and had disallowed the buzz setting. When the ringing stopped, it resumed. His phone was still ringing when the cops arrived.

"Stand back sir."

"Fuck off!"

Luke had Alan's dead face in his hands. The police were cordoning off Alan's landing-spot with white-and-blue plastic. Finally Luke noticed the incessant ringing. He retrieved the phone and declined Max's call. But after he did so, in the shattered screen he saw stacked messages from Nick, from Owen, from Max, from Will, from what seemed to be dozens and dozens of estranged loved ones.

"Stand up," the cop ordered.

Luke stood, staring into his iPhone. New messages popped up every few seconds, too fast for him to read anything more than "*pick up*" and "*Luke!*" and various swear words and multicoloured emojis. The splintered screen went black as Max tried once again to call. Luke swiped right and held the phone to his right ear.

"What?"

"Dude, did you see that comedian who went viral?"

It was Bailey, evidently using Max's phone. Luke had blocked Bailey across every single channel of communication. Over the past months, every time she had tried to use one of Luke's friends' phones to contact him, he had hung up. But Luke did not hang up.

"What?"

"I said, did you see that comedian who went viral?"

"What are you talking about?"

"Luke, you're famous!"

"...Um, this isn't a good time."

"Open Facebook. Open any of your socials. You've gone viral."

"Stand back!" the cop was screaming.

"How?"

"Mark uploaded a video of you impersonating Donald Trump. It's been viewed four—"

"Mark what?"

"It's been viewed four hundred thousand times on YouTube, it's been re-shared by Alex Williamson and Frenchy, Luke, it's got comments on Instagram from all these American comedians, Bert Kreischer, like—*Luke, you're famous!*"

Luke never understood why Mark had uploaded the video. Yet in the weeks that followed, Luke began, reluctantly, to warm to Mark. It was as though Alan's death brought the two of them closer. Luke's mental health stabilised, he returned to his parents' magnificent home, and he opened his heart once more to his younger sister. Mark, Luke, and Bailey all became friends.

The pandemic subsided and the world kept turning. Mark rediscovered his precious singing voice and The Lights played several comeback shows. But they overshot it all by investing far too much money in the recording and production of a self-titled full-length album, which upon release was distributed across all of the important platforms; namely, Spotify, Apple Music, Google Play, and limited-edition waxy-black vinyl. When it became indisputable that the album had bombed, The Lights began to dissolve. The half-white and half-Chinese-Malaysian singer never forgave himself for his role in Alan's death. Mark continued to sing, eventually evolving into a fat and washed-up loser with faded tatts wobbling down his limbs, singing into eternity upon tiny beer-sticky stages in the corners of indifferent Melbourne pubs.

But the Information Age favoured Lucas Weir, who capitalised upon Mark's blind goodness and the resulting virality of Luke's 28 seconds of accidental brilliance. Following Luke's first and spectacularly botched attempt at an open-mic, his career in stand-up comedy flourished, until the rich white boy was a millionaire white man who performed sold-out shows across the world, who was adored by thousands upon thousands of loyal fans, and who had acting roles in dozens of Australian- and Hollywood-produced films. And he remained close with his sister for the rest of their long lives.

Melbourne, Sydney
Dec 2020–Mar 2021

Manufactured by Amazon.com.au
Sydney, New South Wales, Australia